"You'll never see a penny
of my aunt's money!"

Christian's words, when they finally came, shocked
her. She had tried to tell him from the very beginning,
and now, because of her procrastination, it was all
over between them.

"Please," she pleaded, "don't look at me that way. I
thought, I hoped you would understand. I didn't
know your aunt had left me the money. I don't want it!
I only want *you!*"

"I'll fight you in every court in the land. Liars make
poor showings in a courtroom. Now get out!"

SEA GYPSY

Cathy Bissette was seeking sanctuary to heal her broken heart. What she found instead was temptation. One look at sexy Jared Parsons and her heart was suddenly in danger again.

WHISPER MY NAME

Samantha Blakely just couldn't tell her new boss, Christian Delaney, that *she* was *the* Sam Blakely who had inherited his rightful legacy. Worse than losing her job, she risked losing the man of her dreams.

NIGHTSTAR

All at once, Caren Ainsley was a cover-girl sensation and handsome boss Marc Rayven's desire. Caren knew her fame would have its day— but would Marc's love last a lifetime?

WHISPER
MY
NAME

FERN
MICHAELS

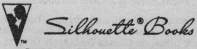

Silhouette® Books

Published by Silhouette Books New York
America's Publisher of Contemporary Romance

SILHOUETTE BOOKS
300 East 42nd St., New York, N.Y. 10017

WHISPER MY NAME

ISBN: 0-373-48273-6

Published Silhouette Books 1981, 1993

Printed in the U.S.A.

Available from Fern Michaels

Sea Gypsy
Whisper My Name
Nightstar

Chapter One

Washington, D.C., in autumn can be one of the most beautiful and exhilarating cities in the world, yet Samantha Blakely walked on lagging feet down Connecticut Avenue, oblivious to the bright gold and orange leaves that cast dappled shadows on the sidewalk. It was unseasonably warm and she felt itchy beneath her heavy sweater jacket, but she was too disheartened to remove it and carry it over her arm. Indian summer, she mused as she kicked at the dry, papery leaves. All Hallow's Eve was tomorrow, and tonight was Mischief Night, when all the neighborhood children would be out wreaking havoc.

Samantha grinned. How well she remembered her own youth and the bars of soap streaking windows and the eggs thrown with gay abandonment. It seemed so long ago, and everything had changed from those remembered nights in a New York neighborhood. Right now, she felt as old as Methuselah and as weary as Job.

She looked up and scanned the numbers on the row of houses and realized she was home at last—the basement apartment she rented from Gemini Delaney.

Samantha fished in her handbag for the bright gold key which hung from a Gucci chain and had been a gift from Gemini, who said that every girl who had her first apartment deserved a Gucci key chain. For some reason the sparkling gold always gave her such a lift, like now, when she was depressed. Gemini always had the answers.

At first Samantha thought she was at the wrong brownstone when she saw a huge orange pumpkin which leaned against a straw facsimile of a scarecrow that leaned beside her door. A giggle found its way to her lips. Gemini again. Gemini Delaney was the oldest little girl Samantha knew, getting her pleasures from the celebration of a second-rate holiday. Sam knew when she made her way to the old lady's door she would find a replica of her own decorations. Wonderful, thoughtful Gemini.

Sam's eye fell to the thin circlet on her wrist as she fit the key in the lock. She would have to hurry or Gemini would start to fret, and she shouldn't be upset, not with her precarious health. All Sam really needed was a quick splash of cold water on her face, a dab of perfume, and a fresh scarf around her neck, preferably one Gemini had given her, and she could skip next door and make it right on time.

Reverently, Sam placed her camera, a Hasselblad and her dearest possession, on the foyer table. Her cinnamon-colored eyes lingered for a moment on the worn case and a single tear formed in the corner of her eye. She wiped at it impatiently. The camera was all she had left of her father, who had been a photo-journalist for CBS News. When he had been killed by terrorists while on an assignment, the camera had been sent along to her by one of his associates. It was all she had left of the man she called Father and who had taught her everything she knew about photography. She couldn't think about that now. Now she had to shift into third gear and get over to Gemini's.

As Sam smoothed the towel over her creamy complexion, she wondered how her feisty but lovable old neighbor had fared with her physician's visit that she knew had taken place early that afternoon. As she ran the brush through her short cropped hair, she realized she had come to love the old woman and would grieve sadly when she was gone.

Don't think about that now, she cautioned herself. Think about how happy Gemini is going to be when the portrait of her nephew, Christian Delaney, was finished. Sam's eyes lightened at the thought and her somber mood lifted. The portrait of Delaney was a piece of her finest work, and she knew it. Running a close second to her love for photography, painting in oils was her most gratifying work. Tonight, after she returned to her own apartment, she would work on the background for a few hours. She hadn't exactly sloughed off working on the portrait, but job hunting was no easy feat, and she was so tired when she returned home at night that all she wanted to do was sleep. Most of the headway she had made on the portrait, which she was copying from a photograph, was done on the weekends. And Gemini had been a real gem about the whole thing. Gemini understood; she always understood.

Sam rummaged on her cluttered dressing table and found the bottle of Chanel No. 5 that had also been a gift from Gemini. She lavishly dabbed on the potent scent. Sam giggled again when she remembered how she and Gemini had been watching television one evening when the commercial came on for the famous perfume. Gemini had laughed uproariously and called the advertisement an obscenity. The next day Neiman-Marcus had delivered the square, elegant box of Chanel to Sam's doorstep. ''I

will feel this way forever." Sam giggled
again, recalling the husky, sensual voice of
the model in the ad as she exited her apartment and locked the door. But only if the
male model emerging from the water was
someone like Christian Delaney. He was the
stuff dreams were made of—impossible
dreams.

Before she had a chance to lift the heavy
bronze knocker, the door was opened by
Gemini's housekeeper. "Miz Delaney is
waiting for you and has your cocktail all
ready. She's a bit upset because her doctor
told her she couldn't have a sherry before
dinner. Right now she's in there sipping the
cats' gin-and-tonic. She don't listen to me,
Miss Blakely. Maybe you can talk to her."

Sam's eyebrows shot upward in alarm.
"Esther, maybe it's just tonic water she's
drinking. Gemini wouldn't disobey the doctor's orders. Where is she?"

Esther snorted indignantly. "It's gin, all
right, and you can just forget about that
tonic water. Them cats are both drunk as two
skunks. She's been giving them sips in their
water dishes. And I can smell gin a mile

away. Miz Delaney is well on her way to getting looped, and I know it." With another snort Esther bobbed her spikey gray head and departed for her own domain—a brick and copper kitchen aromatic with spices and herbs. Sam blinked. She had never seen anyone except Esther who could actually swish an apron the way a stripper tossed her tassels.

If Gemini was drinking, that meant the doctor's news was bad. Gemini could handle anything, even a good drunk. Squaring her shoulders and pasting a smile on her pretty face, Sam bounded into the room and headed straight for the Queen Anne chair where the old lady sat. "Gemini, you are something, do you know that? A pumpkin and a scarecrow. It's perfect. What made you think of it? I love it. How in the world did you get them here?" She knew she was babbling, but she was unable to stop herself. "And that pumpkin is a perfect round ball. When I was a kid, they were always sort of lopsided and... Oh, darn it, Gemini, what did the doctor say?" Sam blurted out as she dropped to her knees at the old woman's feet.

Gemini Delaney straightened her back and patted her blue-white hair, which was carefully arranged down to the last strand. "That doctor is nothing but a spring pup; he's not even dry behind the ears," Gemini said testily, ignoring Sam's question. "For the life of me, I don't know why I put up with him."

"You put up with him because he's the best cardiologist in Washington, D.C., that's why," Sam said softly. "Now, tell me, what did he say?"

"Among other things, he said I was a vicious, cantankerous old woman who should have been put out of her misery ten years ago. What do you think of that?"

Sam forced a smile to her lips. "Did he, now? Or did he say you were a spirited, beautiful lady who should know better than to ignore a doctor's orders?"

Gemini slouched slightly in the yellow velvet chair and muttered, "It might have been something like that, but I really can't remember. This gin robs your brain; you know that. Just look at those stupid cats lying in the fireplace," the old lady snapped.

Sam laughed. "I'd be lying in the fireplace, too, if I drank straight gin. What happened to the tonic water?" she asked, sniffing the glass that rested next to Gemini's chair.

"That fool doctor said if I didn't go into the hospital for his triple bypass I wouldn't last out the week; those were his exact words. That means I have exactly four days left. It's funny how I can remember those words so exactly. Don't you think that's funny, Sam?"

"Hilarious," Sam said past the sob in her throat.

"But there is some good news," the old lady said brightly. "Christian is on his way home. Speaking of Christian, how is the work going on the portrait?"

"Fine, just fine. When I go home tonight, I'm going to work on it. I think I landed a job today. They actually gave me a contract, and I wanted to talk to you about it. I don't know what to do. It's with *Daylight Magazine,* and I think the only reason they even considered me was because of my father."

"Don't be such an upstart that you can't accept help, Sam," Gemini said shortly. "You're an excellent photographer; I've seen your work. Almost as good as your father's. In time you'll be better. Take the job and prove your worth to them. Something else is bothering you. Tell me about it."

Anything to divert the old lady from her grim thoughts, Sam thought worriedly. "It seems to me this contract is tying me up pretty tight and the money they're paying isn't all that good. I know I can't demand or expect anything like the seasoned pros get, but this is barely a living wage. I thought *Daylight* paid well and...oh, Gemini, I don't know what I expected. Look, here's the contract; it's the last two paragraphs that concern me. What do you think?"

The pale, blue-veined hands that reached for the contract were steady, as were the bright, piercing blue eyes. Gemini scanned the printed words and then guffawed. "You're right, child, this contract..."—she sought for just the right word and finally came up with it—"...stinks! Now, this is what you do. You tell them to take out...get me a pencil over there on the desk. Good girl. Now, have them take out paragraph four altogether; demand that paragraph six give you better splits; delete paragraphs nine and ten and..."—the pencil flew over the pages as Sam watched in awe—"...and this is the figure you ask for, and you tell them you won't take a penny less. You tell them that photographs by Orion, that unisex name you insist on using, is one day going to put *Daylight Magazine* right up there with *Time*. You have to be tough and you can't backwater. Tomorrow you march right in there and stand up like your father did. This is what you want. Then you tell him to take it or leave it. Leave your portfolio. Who gave you this contract, anyway?"

"A Mr. Jebard in personnel. Gemini, I don't know if I can do that," Sam said hesitantly.

"Do you believe in yourself, Sam, and in your work?" Gemini said testily.

"Of course. You know I do."

"Then you can do it. I don't want to hear another word. Call me tomorrow after you leave the office. Where's that Esther? She should have announced dinner half an hour ago."

"Here I am, and I didn't announce dinner 'cause I was waiting for you to dry out. You dried out now, Miz Delaney?"

"You old fool, I wasn't even wet," the old lady said fondly to her shiny-faced housekeeper. "Well, don't just stand there, help me get up."

"No, siree, Miz Delaney. The doctor said you was to eat off a tray, and that's exactly what you're going to do."

"And I pay her to torment me like this! Do you believe it?" Gemini sniffed, making no physical effort to move.

Sam smiled weakly, knowing what the light-hearted banter cost the old lady. Esther knew it, too, as she bustled around fluffing first one pillow and then another, finally placing a footstool at Gemini's feet.

"What do you want me to do with them dumb cats lying in the fireplace?" Esther demanded. "It's their dinner time."

"You'll be the death of me yet, Esther. Can't you see they're sleeping? They can eat anytime; leave them alone."

"They ain't sleeping; they're drunk, and when they wake up they're going to have a hangover and I'll have to walk them on a leash. No self-respecting black woman walks cats on a leash. I ain't going to do it, Miz Delaney," Esther muttered as she stomped from the room.

"I worry about her," Gemini said softly as she leaned her frail head back into the softness of the daffodil-colored velvet chair. "She doesn't know it yet, but she's leaving for Seattle. I made all the arrangements this afternoon. I don't want her here when I...when I...she needs a vacation," she said lamely.

Sam's throat constricted at the haunted eyes and the bluish tinge around Gemini's mouth. She forced herself to strive for a light tone. "What has Esther prepared for dinner? Do you know, Gemini?"

"Let's both ask her. Here she comes now with the trays. What have you cooked tonight?"

"The only thing you're allowed to have. Sliced lean chicken and a cup of Jell-O. For Miz Blakely, a sweet potato and a small steak with salad."

The old lady's voice was a shade firmer when she baited the housekeeper still again. "No imagination at all. I'm allowed to have an egg, and you know it. Why didn't you bring me a poached egg?"

"*You* said you could have an egg; the doctor didn't say so. No egg," the housekeeper said adamantly.

Sam's fork was poised midway to her mouth when the soft chime of the telephone bell permeated the room. "I'll get it, Gemini," she said, rising from the chair. "I have it, Esther," she repeated to the housekeeper, who had entered the room at a fast trot. "Hello. Yes, this is Gemini Delaney's residence. Who's calling, please?" Sam covered the receiver with the palm of her hand. Her cinnamon eyes asked a question, but all she said to Gemini was, "It's the overseas operator. Your nephew, Christian Delaney, is calling from Turkey."

The old woman's face lit up momentarily and then settled into grim lines. "Sam, tell him I'm sleeping and that I can't be disturbed. I'll get too emotional, and, right now, I can't handle that." Sam nodded.

"Go ahead, operator, I'll take the call." Sam's heart fluttered wildly. At last, after all these months of working on the portrait Gemini had commissioned, she was finally going to hear the man's voice. It would be deep and husky; she could almost feel it. "Aunt Gemmy, it's Chris here. I've been delayed...*squawk* ... *sputter* ...—*crackle* ... sometime toward ... what's that ... who is this ... *crackle* ..."

"This is Samantha Blakely. I live next door to your aunt.... Hello! Can you hear me ... ?"

"Sputter ... crackle ... squawk ... what man? Where's my ... *crackle* ... home ..."

"Try to get the operator back!" Sam shouted into the crackling phone.

"*Squawk* ... When did you say she would be back?" *Crackle* ... and the line was dead. Sam replaced the phone and shrugged her shoulders. "It was a very poor connection,

Gemini. I could barely make out what he said. I think he's been delayed, but he is coming home. You heard my end. I'm sorry. Don't worry, he'll make it.''

Gemini waved a clawlike hand. ''It's all right. Don't fret, Sam. I'm tired now and I think I'll retire for the night. Call Esther for me and have her help me. Her nose gets out of joint if I don't lean on her every so often. Tell her to bring the phone to my room and plug it in. I have several calls I have to make before I call it a night.''

Sam threw her arms around the thin woman and choked back her tears. ''Not to worry, Gemini. He'll get here in time; I know it.''

''I know it, too, child. You finish your dinner and then run along and work on that portrait so you can have it done by the end of the week. Good night, Sam,'' she said, kissing the young girl's cheek.

''Gemini, thanks for the pumpkin.''

''Later you can make Christian a pie— when he gets here, that is.''

''Of course, I'll be glad to.''

''It's his favorite,'' Gemini said wearily.

Sam obediently finished her dinner as Gemini had instructed. The food, so carefully prepared by Esther, was bland and tasteless on her tongue. As she ate and chewed methodically, Samantha reflected on the unknown well of courage that she had found in herself ever since the truth about Gemini's failing health had become known. Talking so matter-of-factly about death was one of the most difficult things Sam ever had to do. Yet, it was necessary. Gemini demanded it. Confident and pragmatic, Gemini reassured Samantha that death was also a part of living and that eighty-one years was more than enough time for any woman to accomplish a full, exciting life. Sam told herself that Gemini was right, but that didn't help to erase the pain she felt when she thought about the time that the wonderful old woman would no longer be there.

Thanking Esther for dinner, Samantha went back to her own apartment and changed her clothes in favor of a pair of faded old jeans that were streaked with vari-colored paint, and a comfortable, worn shirt. The portrait of Christian Delaney stood on an easel in the spare bedroom in the direct light of the track lamps she had installed. The handsome, intelligent face of Christian Delaney stared back at her from the canvas. The silvery-gray eyes looked out at her from beneath unruly, dark brows and, as always, Sam thought she detected a trace of humor in his otherwise formal and serious pose. Short-cropped hair that held a hint of a wave dipped over his broad brow, and his head was held arrogantly on the thick column of his neck.

Samantha shook herself. It had happened again. Sometimes, when she turned on the light and stood before the portrait of Gemini's nephew, the canvas seemed to breathe life. It was silly, really, for while her painting was true to life and closely followed the photo Gemini had given her, it certainly wasn't so lifelike that she should have these feelings.

Setting a tall stool before the easel and reaching for her palette and various tubes of paint, Sam prepared the quiet browns and umbers she needed for the background and remembered the long, quiet conversations she had shared with Gemini concerning the subject of Christian Delaney. It was possible that Gemini's descriptions of her nephew were so detailed that Samantha imagined she knew the subject of the portrait personally. Even more foolishly, Sam's dreams were more and more often concerned with the real flesh-and-blood Christian, and once or twice she had laughed at herself when she suddenly realized she was actually talking to the dabs of color and paint that created his image on the canvas.

"Stupid fantasies of an old maid," she chided herself as she dabbed and mixed her colors. Yet her gaze was drawn again and again to the eyes that stared back at her, and a tingle of anticipation raced down her spine as she thought that soon, very soon, she would be meeting the real Christian Delaney.

Brush poised in midair, Sam frowned. It wasn't possible... it just couldn't be possible that she was falling in love with the man in the portrait. True, Gemini had spoken so often of him that Sam had the impression that she actually knew him. But the rest was pure foolishness. No self-respecting, halfway intelligent girl who was trying to carve out a career in photo-journalism for herself right here in this day and age could become so mesmerized with a man in a painting that she felt she was falling in love with him!

Her eyes locked with those on the canvas and the anticipated tingle danced the length of her spine. "Foolish!" Samantha scolded herself as she slammed down her palette and concentrated on the background of the portrait, purposely refusing to permit her eyes to stray to the handsome, compelling features of her subject.

Chapter Two

The heavy portfolio tucked under her arm, Sam waited patiently for a bus at the corner that would drop her off at the *Daylight* door. Inside her purse, in the zipper compartment, was a neatly typed list of corrections for her new contract. Would the man called Mr. Conway be amenable to the changes she was going to request, or would he laugh and tell her to peddle her work somewhere else?

Sam settled back in her hard seat on the bus and willed herself to relax. She felt good and at this precise moment in time she felt she exuded confidence. For some strange reason she always felt that way after a few hours of work on Christian Delaney's portrait. The work last night had gone well, and Gemini would be pleased. Even Christian Delaney, if he ever saw the finished product, would find himself hard pressed to find fault with her work. What was he like? Gemini had said he stood well over six feet and had steel-gray eyes that saw through a person to the very soul. At Gemini's death he was to inherit the family-owned business, and at that time he would settle down and raise a family, or so Gemini hoped. Gemini had said he was strong willed, yet gentle and vulnerable, but she hadn't explained how or why he was vulnerable, but had said someday Samantha would find out for herself. It would be easy to fall in love with Christian Delaney, and if Samantha admitted the truth, even to herself, here on this noisy bus, she was already half in love with his likeness.

"K Street," the bus driver called loudly to be heard above the busy chattering.

Sam slid from her seat and walked to the middle of the bus and waited for the double doors to swish open. She held the portfolio tightly and settled her canvas shoulder bag more comfortably on her shoulder. She made the half-block in minutes and walked through the revolving door. "Mr. Conway, here I come, ready or not," she muttered, pressing the Up button. Her heart fluttered wildly when the elevator door opened and she squeezed past the departing occupants. She pressed number 16 and leaned weakly against the wall. Did she have the nerve? Could she do what Gemini told her to do? Of course she could. She had come this far, and besides, how would she ever explain her lack of courage to Gemini?

Sam's eyes did a slow once-over of the elaborate reception area and came to rest on a lacquered china doll-like woman sitting behind a desk with an intercom system at her fingertips. "I'd like to see Mr. Conway, please," Sam said in a voice she didn't recognize.

The receptionist spoke softly, her voice a musical chime. "May I ask your name?"

"Samantha Blakely. I'm a photographer and I work under the name Orion."

"You're Orion!" the tiny woman exclaimed. "May I say that I saw the pictures you took of the boat people and...and they were just...you captured... What can I say? I liked them."

Sam literally gasped. "Did you really like them? I always feel that I did well if just one person says so. Thank you, thank you so much for the compliment."

The other woman smiled. "Mr. Conway is busy, but I'll interrupt him. He's just putting in his office." She gave Sam a wicked wink and pressed a small white button. She spoke softly and motioned with her hand. "Just give him time to put away his golf club and get behind his desk," she whispered. Sam let her left eye close and walked slowly to a heavy oak door. At the receptionist's nod, she opened the door and then closed it softly behind her. *Here goes nothing*, she said silently as she walked forward to a monstrous desk.

A pink, balding-type man rose from behind the desk and held out his hand. "Charlie Conway," he said jovially, "and you're Orion. Sit down and take a load off your feet. What can I do for you?"

Samantha licked at dry lips and remembered Gemini's words. "Look, Mr. Conway, I'm a good photographer—not the best, but good. Your Mr. Jebard offered me a contract yesterday to work for this magazine. I led him to believe I would sign it, and I had every intention of signing it until I read it more thoroughly. What I'm trying to say is, it's not satisfactory. I'd like to tell you what I would like, and then perhaps we could compro—then perhaps we could come to terms. On second thought, Mr. Conway, I can't compromise or come to terms." Before the man behind the desk could utter another word, Sam was reading off her list of corrections to the contract. "Not a penny less, Mr. Conway. I'll be honest with you. I want this job more than I ever wanted anything, and I know I'll be an asset to your staff, but you have to be fair, too." Sam leaned back, a fine beading of perspiration dotting her forehead. She waited.

"You got it. Listen, kid, what do you do for an encore?"

"Got it? You mean you...you agree to my terms and I don't do an encore?"

"I don't think so. You shot your load the first time around. Look, kid, I knew your old man and I liked him. You've got the same kind of guts he had. There aren't too many people who would march in here and make demands, not even the seasoned pros. You've got guts, and I like that. Your old man and me, we went through some rough times back in the old days. I bunked with him for three solid months in Beirut, when neither one of us could take a bath in all that time. We remained friends, and let me tell you something. Your old man smelled about as raunchy as I did when we finally made our way home. I heard he died a couple of years ago. I'm sorry. He used to talk about you and that Brownie Hawkeye you had. He was proud of you, kid."

Sam was stunned. "Mr. Conway, are you giving me the job just because you knew my father?"

"No! You said Jebard gave you the job yesterday. I just cleaned up his contract for him. What kind of camera are you using?"

"My dad's Hasselblad."

"Kid, that camera has a soul. Don't ever lose it. You using your dad's Leitz lenses?"

"Every last one of them." Sam smiled.

"Looks like we're in business, then. You can start work Monday morning. I'll see what's on the roster, and your first assignment will be ready whenever you are. Welcome aboard, Orion," he said, holding out his hand. "I'm glad you're using your old man's handle. Old cameramen never die, that kind of thing," Conway said sheepishly. "And, kid, call me Charlie. Oh, one other thing—if that's your portfolio, leave it here. Our new president will be in Monday, too, and I'm sure he's going to want to check over our newest addition. I'll give you a good buildup, kid."

"Mr. Con—Charlie, thank you, thank you for everything, but mostly, thanks for telling me about my dad. Maybe someday we can get together and swap stories. I'd really like to hear about some of your experiences."

"I'd like that, too, Orion."

Sam walked on air all the way back to her apartment. She felt good. Thank God for Gemini. She was supposed to call her from the office and let her know how she made out. Darn, she thought wretchedly, how could she have forgotten something so important? A taxi. She would take a taxi and get home as fast as she could and tell Gemini in person.

She was too late. . . .

On the day of the funeral, it was fitting that it should rain. Complying with Gemini Delaney's wishes, the services were simple and private. Esther had been given the name of the law firm that handled the old woman's affairs, and the lawyers had taken it from there.

Flowers arrived at the funeral home, and notes of condolence came to Christian Delaney, who still had not returned home. When Samantha questioned Esther as to how Mr. Delaney could be reached, the dark-skinned woman shook her head and shrugged. "All I know, Miz Blakely, is that those lawyers are trying to reach him. But you know Miz Delaney never waited for no man. Her instructions were to have the funeral and get it over with quickly. She used to say that life was for the living, and that the dead don't deserve much more than a passing respect."

Sam smiled bleakly. How like Gemini that was. Never thinking of herself. Gemini was a giver, not a taker. Samantha was aware of the old woman's affection for her nephew and what a comfort his presence would have been during those last days. And yet Gemini hadn't summoned him home. Even though Gemini had been so forgiving concerning her nephew's lack of interest and understanding, Sam wasn't so certain she could.

At the yawning grave site, Samantha gave way to the tears that were building inside her. The rain slashed down unmercifully. The only other mourners present, as per Gemini's instructions for privacy, were Esther, several friends from the neighborhood where Gemini had lived for the past twenty years, and a wizened old gentleman in a shabby, black raincoat and a slouch hat whom Sam rightly suspected was one of Gemini's lawyers.

As the last prayers were murmured and silent goodbyes were said, Samantha found it increasingly difficult to choke back her tears. She knew she had to look forward, not backward. She would grieve for Gemini in private, late at night. For now, she had to carry on with her life just as Gemini expected. She mustn't betray the confidence that Gemini had had in her. She would give her best to *Daylight Magazine* and prove her own worth.

Esther and Samantha rode back to the brownstone together, each silent with her own thoughts. When they approached Connecticut Avenue, Esther dried her eyes on her handkerchief and blew her nose. "I'll be taking a late-afternoon plane to Seattle, Miz Blakely. I've written down my address." She dug in her handbag and withdrew a slip of paper. "If there's anything you need and I can help, that's where I'll be."

"Thank you, Esther," Sam said warmly, suddenly realizing how much she was going to miss the housekeeper's warm concern. "You've been a good friend, and I'm going to miss you."

"You won't have time to miss anybody, Miz Blakely. Those two cats Miz Delaney left to you are going to keep you busy enough. Why, you'll be working at your magazine just to keep those two devils in gin."

The two women laughed, each remembering Gemini's devotion to her cats.

"Tell me, Esther, did Gemini name them Gin and Tonic before or after she discovered their penchant for the drink?"

"Miz Blakely, just like everybody else who ever had anything to do with Miz Delaney, they just lived up to what she expected of them!"

Alone that evening, Sam automatically switched on the track lighting in the spare bedroom, intending to work on the portrait of Christian Delaney. Fresh tears stung her eyes as she realized that Gemini would never see the finished product. Still, Gemini had commissioned the portrait and, in fact, had paid her in advance. The money she had given Sam had gone for expenses while job hunting. That advance had meant that Samantha had been able to hold out for the best job she could land, instead of being forced by dwindling finances to grab the first thing that came along. Her commitment to Gemini had been to complete the portrait, and complete it she would. Then she would have it sent on to Christian Delaney with a note of explanation.

Lifting her eyes to the easel, her gaze fell on the face of Christian Delaney. She knew it was only her imagination, but there seemed to be a calculating look about the silver-gray eyes. Samantha bit her lip. The one person Gemini had loved more than anyone else in the world had been absent from the private funeral ceremonies.

Tonight was definitely not the right time to work on the portrait, she decided as she switched off the light, and she wondered if she was more disappointed for Gemini than angry. One of the cats snaked around her ankles and purred loudly. ''All right, all right. I promised Gemini I would take care of you, and I will. Let's go into the kitchen, and I'll warm up some milk for the three of us.''

Just as Sam was dressing for work on Monday morning, the doorbell shrilled. Startled, she laid down the hairbrush and raced to the door. Who could be ringing her bell so early on a Monday morning? She glanced at the sunburst clock in the living room as she opened the door. It was only seven-ten. "Registered letter for Sam Blakely," a tired-looking older man said quietly.

Sam frowned. Now, who would be sending her a registered letter? Please, God, don't let it be the magazine saying they had second thoughts. She scribbled her name and closed the door. Hmm. Hartford, Masterson, Quinlan, Jacobsen, and Zigenback, Attorneys at Law, followed by a prestigious address on Wisconsin Avenue. With trembling hands, Sam slit open the envelope and quickly scanned the contents. She was to be present in Addison Hartford's office at twelve noon for the reading of Gemini Delaney's will. Sam grinned. Gemini wasn't leaving anything to chance. The two cats,

Gin and Tonic, were to come to her for care. Gemini was making it legal. It wasn't so bad; she could take a taxi and still be back in the office by one o'clock. She stuffed the crisp, crackling legal letter into her purse and resumed her dressing.

After setting a small bowl of water, a second of tonic water, *sans* gin, and a dish of cat food on the kitchen floor, Sam was ready to leave for her first day at her new job. She felt good and knew she looked just as good in her tailored navy pants suit. At the last minute she crushed a matching beret on her head, covering her short-cropped curls. Her camera case over one shoulder and a smart burgundy shoulder bag completed her outfit.

Her heart skipped a beat and then steadied as her eyes fell on the orange pumpkin. *Don't think of that now. Today is the first day of the rest of your life,* her mind mumbled over and over.

She reached the corner just as a bus pulled to a stop. She boarded and settled herself for the short ride downtown. No worries, no problems. She had given her word to Gem-

ini, and she would keep it. The cats were hers
and she would see to their proper care. She
smiled as she remembered what they were
doing when she left. Gin had found a spot in
the clothes hamper and had managed to
wrap himself in a bright scarlet towel, while
Tonic had dragged her boots from a heavy
box and settled herself half-in and half-out
of her fur-lined left boot. They were making
themselves right at home, but she promised
herself that she was going to put both of
them on the wagon and turn them into re-
spectable cats if it was the last thing she did.

"K Street!" the bus driver shouted loudly.
Sam followed the other debarking passengers and headed straight for the *Daylight*
offices.

Her co-workers turned out to be a friendly
group of people. Easygoing, willing to help,
and an endless supply of stories to tell. By
eleven o'clock she had had the grand tour,
been assigned a cubbyhole of an office, been
introduced to the supply room with wall-to-
wall film supplies, and had been informed
that her meeting with the publisher and
president was set for two o'clock. A memo

on her clean desk also informed her she was to report to Charlie Conway at three o'clock for her first assignment.

Sam busied herself for another forty-five minutes by hanging up some of her favorite shots on the small cork bulletin board that came with every cubbyhole. She stood back to admire her handiwork. Photos by Orion. It did have a ring to it. Dad would be proud if he could see her now.

If she half-raised herself from her chair and stretched her neck, she could just make out the bank of clocks hanging on the newsroom wall. She did both and then reset her watch. Time to leave for Hartford, Masterson, Quinlan, Jacobsen, and Zigenback.

Sam waited patiently in the dusty, fern-decorated room of the old, prestigious law firm. Eventually, a middle-aged secretary appeared and crooked her finger in Sam's direction, which she took to mean she was to follow. Monstrous double doors creaked shut on dry hinges as Sam crossed fifty feet of worn carpeting. She looked around. Old furniture, bookshelves filled with legal tomes, and a desk the size of a billiard table with a row of diamond-shaped windows took up one corner of the room. To the left of the heavy-looking bookcases were two leather chairs, one in burgundy cracked leather and the other black. A brass lamp and a spittoon ashtray rested on a dusty table. The only words Sam could think of were "old" and "dry," just like the aging man behind the desk. Sam stared down at the wizened gentleman with the sparse white hair and pince-nez and recognized him from the cemetery. She held out her hand, which he ignored. "I'm..."

"Sam Blakely," chirped a reedy voice. "Sit down and let me read you Mrs. Delaney's will. Mr. Delaney can't be here, so we might as well proceed. My eyes aren't what they used to be, and I can't seem to...I don't know where that infernal will is," the old man fretted. "It doesn't make any difference; I know what was in it. Someone will send you a letter confirming what I'm about to tell you. Settle back, Mr. Blakely, and... now, where did I...never mind."

"Mr. Hartford, it's not Mr. Blakely—I'm Ms. Blakely. Mr. Hartford, is your hearing aid turned on?'' Sam asked as she noticed a braided wire that ran into his shirt collar.

The old man ignored her words and laced his fingers together. "If I recall rightly, what Gemini's will said was that you, Sam Blakely, are to receive the dividends from fifty-one percent of the family-owned stock for ninety days. After the ninety days an addendum to the will is to be read—if I can find it," the old man said peevishly. "It seems to me that you can't vote, but I'll have one of the younger men check that out and get back to you."

Sam gasped. "Mr. Hartford, are you sure you don't have me mixed up with someone else? I was supposed to get the cats—cats, Mr. Hartford. Mr. Hartford, what about the cats?" Sam shouted.

"Those drunken animals! It's a disgrace and a sin the way Gemini turned them into alcoholics. There's no need for you to shout, Blakely. The battery in my hearing aid is low, but I assure you I can hear just fine. There was something about the cats in the will. A neighbor, I believe, was to be entrusted with their care, plus a cash annuity to pay for their alcoholic comfort. I'll have to check that out.''

"I'm that neighbor—I'm Samantha Blakely. Never mind, Mr. Hartford, just send me the letter. I have the cats and they're being well cared for,'' Sam said wearily as she watched the frail attorney fidget with the button in his ear.

"Oh, pish and tush, this infernal gadget never works when I want it to work,'' the old man muttered. "It's no never mind. May I say I admire that hat you're wearing, Mr. Blakely? I had one quite similar to it when I was a boy. Everything's gone now—the hat, my hearing, my eyesight. I'm retired, you know, and just came into the office today because Gemini and I were friends for sixty years. It was the least I could do. I'll keep in touch, Mr. Blakely.''

Should she protest again and hope to get through to the old man, or should she just leave? Sam shrugged. What was the use? Before she could button her jacket she heard loud snores permeate the room. No use at all. In the waiting room with the dusty ferns and threadbare carpet, Sam looked around.

All the doors were closed and there was no sign of anyone. Probably taking a nap. She giggled as she tiptoed out of the office and hailed a cab.

There must be a mistake, and, hopefully, it would be righted in the form of a letter. Fond as Gemini was of her, she certainly wouldn't leave her a controlling interest in her business. After all, hadn't Gemini said that her nephew was the sole heir? And, come to think of it, just what was Gemini's business? She had never said, and Sam had never asked. Ninety days and then an addendum was to be read. What exactly did that mean? It was all a mistake, and one she couldn't worry about now. If she was lucky, she could catch a sandwich in the snack bar at the office and freshen up before she was to meet the new president of *Daylight Magazine*.

Sam knocked smartly on the door of the president's office promptly on the stroke of two o'clock. A terse, cold "Come" made her draw in her breath. He sounded like an ogre, an angry ogre. Squaring her shoulders, she entered the office and walked over to the desk where a man was shouting into the phone, the high back of his chair turned toward her. Impatiently, he waved a hand in the air, motioning for her to sit.

"Just what does that mean? Mr. Hartford, I have great respect for your age and your ability, but how in the name of heaven did you allow Gemini to be duped by some . . . some gigolo named . . . what was the name . . . ? Sam Blakely? You were Aunt Gem's closest friend and should have seen to her last needs and wishes. Well, it won't hold water, I can tell you that. There is no such thing as an unbreakable will. I'll break it, and I'll break the neck of Sam-whatever-his-name-is. Find him, Mr. Hartford, and I'll show you a chiseler out to bilk old ladies. Gemini must not have been of sound mind. What do you mean, she drew up the will herself? Don't give me any sermons, Hartford, I want that will contested. I'm the heir, the only heir. No, I don't begrudge Gemini's gifts, but I do intend to find that weasel, Sam Blakely, and wring his neck. Do you hear me, Hartford? Don't you pay out one cent of those dividends. Get it through your head I'm the heir—the *only* heir. No, not for later, for now. How old is this Sam Blakely, anyway? Twenty-three! What time was he in your office? You should have kept him there till I could get there! Hartford, I don't care what kind of hat he had on! I'm advising you now that I'm going to break that will long before the addendum is to be read. You're right I want to see a copy of the will!'' Silence. ''In that case, Mr. Hartford, I won't just break his neck—I'll kill him before I let him prey on some other poor, unsuspecting old lady. Of course I don't mean it. He'll never be the same, though, I can assure you of that. After work I'll stop by your home and pick up a copy. Do you still reside in Georgetown? Around seven, then.''

Sam stifled a gasp. Good heavens, it wasn't possible, was it? He couldn't be...he was! The new president and publisher of *Daylight Magazine* was Christian Delaney, Gemini's nephew. Sam's head reeled as she stared at her new boss. How could this happen to her? And why hadn't Gemini told her? Sam remembered the old woman telling her that Christian would inherit the family business when she passed on, but she hadn't known that publishing was their business. A lump formed first in the pit of her stomach and then worked its way up to her throat. And to think he actually thought she had bilked dear, sweet Gemini! Well, she would just tell him he was mistaken; that was all there was to it. Mr. Hartford was a different story, but this man wasn't wearing a hearing aid. Talk about your comedy of errors. How could a reasonably intelligent man like Christian Delaney jump to conclusions like this? He was going to turn around and she would tell him. Oh, how had she ever gotten into this mess? It was so simple, if this lump would just go away, she might be able to get the words out. Fifty-one percent of the stock was going to her, and that meant the man with his back to her only had forty-nine percent. Would it make a difference if she was male or female? He thought she was a gigolo. *Gemini, do you know what you did?*

The man turned abruptly, the phone clenched in his powerful-looking fist. Slowly, deliberately, he replaced it and spoke, his words chips of ice. "Orion, isn't it?" Not bothering to wait for her reply, he continued: "I must apologize for the conversation you just heard. It's a family problem and I allowed myself to get out of control for a few minutes. I've looked at your portfolio and I liked what I saw."

She was supposed to say something, acknowledge the compliment. "Thank... thank you," she said lamely.

"You're new, according to Charlie Conway, but then so am I—in the capacity of president, that is. Until recently, I've been in charge of foreign publications and keeping our diplomatic doors open overseas. We should get along fine since we're both starting out at the same time. You bear with me and I'll bear with you. What do you say?"

His eyes were just as beautiful as in the photograph. "That... th-that would be fi-fine." Fifty-one percent, fifty-one percent, fifty-one percent! her mind shrieked silently.

"I wanted to spend some time with you and go over your portfolio, but I have some personal business I must take care of start-

ing right now. How would you like to have
dinner with me? I have an evening appointment, but I think instead I'll take care of the
matter now, before I get any hotter under the
collar. Let's say Jour et Nuit. Are you familiar with it? No? M Street at Thirtieth in
Georgetown. You'll like it—fireside dining,
and the food is served Continental style.
Very impressive wine list. I guarantee it.
Well," he said abruptly, "will you have dinner with me?"

Sam's mind raced. "Of...of c-course."

"Do you always stutter?" Christian Delaney asked, frowning.

"Well...I...I...this is my...my first
day...and...and I never met a president
before."

Christian Delaney laughed, a deep, rich
baritone. She knew, she just knew he would
laugh like that. "I have news for you; I've
never been a president before, either, and
I'm not all that sure I'll be any good at the
job."

"Of course you will. You look just the
way a president should look," Sam babbled

and then was instantly embarrassed at her words. She flushed.

"Amazing! Absolutely amazing!" Christian said in a voice that resembled awe. "A woman today who can still blush. I like that, Orion. You've got yourself a date with a president." The steel-gray eyes were merry and showed just a shade of devilment. Did presidents do things like "that." If the president was a man, he did. The flush darkened, to Christian Delaney's amusement. "Look, do you think you could meet me at the restaurant? I don't usually make my dates do this, but I'm going to be running late, and... and I want to get to know you better."

Before or after you kill me? her whirling brain questioned. "I don't mind, Mr. Delaney."

"I think I'm going to like you, Orion. A woman who stutters because I'm a president and who can still blush and who says she doesn't mind meeting me at the restaurant. Do you even check the prices on the menu?"

An invisible broom handle stiffened Sam's spine. "As a matter of fact, I do. And," she said airily, "I don't eat much."

"Seven o'clock. And I was complimenting you, whether you know it or not. I appreciate promptness."

Was he mocking her? "I'll be on time."

"Are you one of those women who dawdle and pick at their food, or do you eat to enjoy?"

"I know what fork to use and I've never been known to use my fingers. I usually eat fast because I'm hungry and my dad taught me never to leave anything on my plate. Did I leave anything out?" she asked, a cutting edge to her voice. "And," she said, holding up her hand, "I do not pick up the check."

The silvery-gray eyes narrowed to slits. "We'll discuss that over dinner. That's a smart-looking outfit you're wearing. More than suitable for the restaurant."

"Yes, I know. I've been to a restaurant before, Mr. Delaney. I won't embarrass you."

Christian Delaney inclined his head slightly as Sam left the office. At the door

Sam turned and almost missed the speculative look in Christian Delaney's eyes. Those gray eyes that stared back at her every day from the portrait. She said nothing, but merely closed the door quietly behind her.

Once again Sam craned her neck to stare at the clock. Another half-hour till her meeting with Charlie Conway and her first assignment. Where would it be, and what would it be? Might as well go to the supply room and stock up on film and other supplies while she was waiting. But first she would get a cup of the rancid coffee the cameramen called ambrosia and think a little. She really had to decide what she was going to do. Christian Delaney was no fool. Gemini was right—he saw straight through to your soul. She didn't like the thought and felt frightened. What would he do when he found out Orion was Sam Blakely? Would Charlie Conway tell him before she could? Not likely; nor would the other cameramen and newsmen. They were introduced to her as Orion, and first names held. As far as they were concerned, that was her handle and they cared nothing for her legal name;

and, if by some chance someone mentioned it, they would promptly forget it; it was the nature of the trade.

Why was she so edgy, so frightened? She hadn't done anything wrong. A mistake had been made, and as long as she didn't accept any money from Gemini's estate, she was in the clear. A sinking feeling gripped her innards. She had every reason to be frightened. Christian Delaney was ruthless and without sentiment. Business always came first. Hadn't he proved this by putting business ahead of being with Gemini in her last hours? Europe was only ten or eleven hours away by air. He hadn't even come to the funeral. Gemini's estate was business of the first order. Why should she expect him to be any less ruthless and understand the mistake that had been made? Surely, Christian Delaney wouldn't want the alcoholic cats. That issue she would fight him on simply because she and Gemini had many discussions and she had given the old lady her word that she would care for the animals. She would honor her promise no matter what.

Gemini—kind, gentle, feisty Gemini, owning *Daylight Magazine*. It was unbelievable. No wonder Gemini had known what to tell her to ask for in the contract. "Don't be such an upstart that you can't accept help." Those were Gemini's words. So what if she used the unisex name? So what if Gemini helped her with the contract? And so what if Gemini put in a good word for her? She was a darned good photographer, and she would prove it or die trying. There was no way she would let Gemini down, not now, not ever.

Sam stretched her neck. Five minutes to three and she hadn't gotten any coffee, after all. Her musings had taken up a good twenty-five minutes. Now it was time to meet with Charlie Conway and see what she would be doing and where she was going.

Evil, blue-gray smoke as thick as marshmallows greeted Sam as she rapped smartly on Charlie Conway's door and entered. Coughing and sputtering, Sam collapsed against the wall and burst into laughter as she waved her arms to ward off the obnoxious fumes. "Now I know where my dad caught his habit. I didn't think there were two people in the whole world who would find the same cigar and actually smoke it."

"Let me tell you something, kid," Charlie said, working the fat, brown cylinder between his teeth. "These cee-gars were the only thing that kept me and your old man sane during some darned fool uprising in South America. We decided early on that if we were meant to be killed, it wasn't going to be by some guerrilla, but by a fifteen-cent cee-gar. They're up to thirty cents now. Would you believe it? You can open the window if you want," Charlie said generously.

"I wouldn't think of it," Sam retorted as she dabbed at her watering eyes.

Charlie worked the cigar to the side of his mouth and fished around his cluttered desk for a sheaf of official-looking papers. "Okay, Orion, you're going to partner with Ramon Gill. In case you don't know it, he's got the fastest pencil in the east. He's a good man—lascivious, but good. You can handle it. If he gets out of hand, threaten to take a shot of his left profile; he hates that. You're going to California tonight. Here's your

plane ticket, along with some expense
money. Right now, that fire raging in the
canyon is nothing more than a brush affair,
but in another twelve hours it's going to be
the biggest bonfire you ever saw. I want you
and Ramon to be the first ones there.''

Sam nodded. It never occurred to her to
ask the man seated behind the desk how he
knew the brush fire was going to rage. He
was a newsman, and if he said it was going
to go, then it was going to go. Newsmen had
a sixth sense, and that was good enough for
her.

''I want you and Ramon right there in the
front Don't be afraid of a little soot and
ash. Just get me good footage. You got
that?'' Sam nodded. ''And don't let some
jackass try to ward you off because you're a
woman.   Around   here   you're   Orion,
cameraperson. Is that clear?'' Sam nodded.
''Well, what are you waiting for?''

Sam grimaced. ''I was sort of hoping for
a 'good luck' or 'take care' or something.''

''You make your own luck, and if you
have any brains, you'll take care of yourself. My wishing you anything isn't going to

make a bit of difference. Hang in there, kid, and I'll see you back here in three days, give or take a few either way."

Before she left the office, Sam phoned Ramon Gill and arranged to meet him at National Airport at eleven o'clock. They would take the "red-eye" together, getting in to Los Angeles in the wee hours of the morning.

She took another taxi she couldn't afford back to the apartment to pick up the cats for boarding. Time for a quick shower and time to pack a duffel. Then dinner with Christian Delaney. Sometime between the appetizer and dessert she would tell him *she* was the Sam Blakely mentioned in Gemini's will. With a little luck she could run out of the restaurant before he fired her, and she could at least get one assignment for *Daylight* under her belt. She had to make it perfectly clear to him that she had known nothing about the will. Also, she'd make him understand she never knew Gemini owned *Daylight Magazine*. Her heart pounded all through the taxi ride and only returned to normal when she exited at her doorstep.

Her hand trembled as she fit the gold key into the lock. The phone in the living room was shrilling as she closed the door and threw the dead bolt. She raced across the room only to hear the dial tone as she placed the receiver to her ear. Whoever it was would call back if it was important.

First things first. She stripped down, showered and redressed. Makeup went on sparingly, as did a dab of perfume. She packed heavy twill pants and sweat shirts along with a week's change of underwear. Toilet articles in a leather case were next, along with a pair of hiking boots. In this business you traveled light and smelled a lot.

Now the cats. She called them and, as usual, they ignored her. She'd have to do what Gemini did. Craftily, she bent down to the liquor cabinet in the corner and managed to clink the gin bottle and tonic water at the same time. One cat was on her shoulder, and the other twined himself around her leg. "Look, guys, this was a fake. There isn't enough in either bottle for a shot. You're a disgrace. The vet isn't going to cater to your problems, so let's go on the wagon right now. A few days of milk will do you both a lot of good." Both cats looked at her disdainfully and swept out of the room, their lush tails straight out to show their disapproval. "Come on, now, you have to get into your basket," she said, chasing them and scooping both up at the same time. "I don't want to hear a peep out of either one of you. You're sober now and you're going to stay that way." Both cats hissed their anger as she snapped the lid of the carryall and lugged it to the front door. Now, where was the vet Gemini had used for the cats? Quickly, she flipped through her address book till she found the name of the animal hospital. Rockville! A fast look at the sunburst clock told her if she avoided the rush-hour traffic, she might make it. She still had the keys to Gemini's vintage Mercedes. As much as she disliked doing it, she would have to use the car.

The cats hissed and clawed at the wicker as she lugged them to the garage at the rear of the brownstone. She slid open the doors and placed the cats on the floor in the back of the car. A yowl of outrage made the fine hairs on the back of her neck stand on end. "Both of you be quiet. I can't drive with all that screeching," she called over her shoulder as she maneuvered the heavy car down the alley and onto Connecticut Avenue. Sam drove fast, her eyes glued to the rearview mirror for any sign of the city's finest. Walter Reed Medical Center on the right. She was making progress.

Sam popped a stale mint into her mouth as she swung north on Georgia Avenue and made her way to the Capital Beltway. The Interstate green read: NORTHERN VIRGINIA. Sam took the second right, looping back to merge westbound with Interstate Maryland 495. Noticing a gap in the middle lane, Sam pushed down on the directional lever and eased into the slow-moving traffic. She heard the snap of the wicker lid as her eyes sighted the Mormon Temple. To Sam's eye it looked like a glacial cathedral sculpted from a massive chunk of ice. The cats were loose and hopping onto the front seat. Playfully, they hissed and scratched at the plush seats to celebrate their freedom.

Twenty minutes later Sam stood at the reception desk in the vet's office, the heavy basket next to her on the countertop. Loud hisses and snarls swept through the office. Quickly, Sam explained who she was and the situation with the cats.

"Miss Blakely," the receptionist said, a look of panic on her face, "the doctor can't treat Mrs. Delaney's cats. He simply refuses. The last time they were here we all had to go on tranquilizers. They're disruptive. We couldn't determine what their problem was and decided they were just riddled with neuroses. I'm sorry, really sorry."

It was Sam's turn to panic. They had to take the cats. "If I tell you what's wrong with these cats, will you take them?"

The receptionist inched away from the counter. Her eyes were shifty as she stared at the noisy basket. "Well, that depends on whether the condition is treatable. I'm Dr. Barstow's wife, and I can't have my husband upset with those animals like the last time. What is it?" she asked fearfully.

"They're alcoholics."

"Alcoholics?" Mrs. Barstow said stupidly.

"Yes. I've got them on the wagon, but I can see now that I'll have to wait till I get back to dry them out. Just give them some gin and tonic and they're as docile as two kittens. Believe me," Sam pleaded as she made her way to the door, hoping against hope that the woman wouldn't call her back and demand she take the hissing cats with her. "I'll pick them up in a week, sooner if I get back before then. Thank you, thank you so much," she babbled as she ran from the office.

If she didn't hit traffic, she could make her seven o'clock appointment for dinner with Christian Delaney right on schedule. She prayed silently all the way back to the city and didn't draw a safe breath till she hit Wisconsin Avenue. She drove through Rock Creek Park, admiring the rich colors of late autumn, silently congratulating herself on a job well done. The cats were safe, for the moment, and she had Gemini's car back, secure in its space in the double garage. Carefully, she locked the garage and slipped the keys into her purse. Along with her confession, she would turn the keys over to Christian Delaney. Surely, he wouldn't mind that she had used his aunt's car for the trip to Rockville. After all, it was for the cats, not a joy ride.

She raced around the corner to her apartment. She dialed and waited for the crackly voice of the taxi dispatcher to tell her how long she would have to wait for a cab. "Three minutes," she was told.

Sam heard the phone ring as she locked the door behind her. Should she go back and answer? She was saved the decision when a blue and white cab slid up to the curb. Whoever it was would have to call back later. A lot later.

The cab ground to a smooth stop in front of the restaurant just as a yellow Jaguar cut in front of it. Christian Delaney emerged from the low-slung sports car just as Sam paid the driver.

Christian Delaney eyed the worn duffel bag and the heavy camera case. Sam explained and was surprised to see her escort frown. "It's no problem; you can check both of them at the cloakroom."

"You're wrong. I'll check the duffel, but this camera never leaves my side."

"It must make a cold bedfellow." Christian grinned as the maître d' showed them to a cozy table near the monstrous fireplace. "What will you have to drink, Orion?"

"Scotch on the rocks." Sam watched as Christian's eyebrows shot up in surprise. What did he think she was going to order, a Shirley Temple? He ordered the same thing for himself and then lit a cigarette. "That's the second time I've surprised you in the space of a few minutes. Why?"

Christian answered bluntly, "I was surprised that Conway assigned you to cover the pictorial side of the fire, and I didn't expect you to order Scotch—it's a man's drink."

"Two sexist remarks in one sentence." Sam grinned. "I don't see what my gender has to do with my ability to photograph a fire, and I happen to like Scotch."

"Well said." Christian grinned, showing a flash of strong white teeth. "What time does your plane leave? Who's the journalist? Normally, I would know all about this assignment, but as I told you, I had family business to take care of this afternoon and didn't go back to the office after lunch.''

Sam was glad she had both hands around the squat glass in front of her. She blinked and felt her heart resume its normal beat. ''And did you settle your family business?'' Was that calm, casual voice hers?

''No, I didn't.'' Christian's tone was vehement. ''If there's one thing I cannot and will not abide, it is professional, slick con artists who prey on defenseless old ladies. Tomorrow, I'm hiring the best private detective firm in the city to track down that slick weasel, and when I find him I'm going to...'' Sam gulped and wished she could drown herself in the amber fluid she was holding. Now. She should tell him now! Samantha opened her mouth, forcing the words to her lips. But before she could utter a sound, he interrupted.

''I'm sorry. That's the second time I allowed family matters to intrude. Pleasantries only from now on. Tell me how you came to be a photo-journalist.''

Sam relaxed. This was familiar ground and she was comfortable. What seemed like hours later she glanced at her watch, dreading to see what numbers the hands rested on. Soon it would be time to go; and, suddenly, she didn't want to leave this man's presence—not now, not ever. She must tell him now, before she left. She couldn't continue playing this game of hide-and-seek. In essence, she was deceiving him, and that deceit was making everything a lie—her job, the assignment, this dinner, even the way Christian's eyes were smiling into hers. Her confession would change everything. Samantha gulped, feeling a shudder run through her. Taking a deep breath, she began: "Christian, I must tell . . ."

Christian's voice was cool, almost mocking when he interrupted: "That's the third time I've seen you glance at your watch. Am I boring you?"

Sam stared at the man across from her and flushed a deep crimson. "On . . . on the contrary. I just . . . just realized that . . . that it's getting late and I'm going to . . . to have to leave . . . soon. I'm having such a good time

I don't . . . I don't want to leave," she said honestly and could have bitten her tongue the minute the words were out. "But before I do, I have to tell . . ."

Christian leaned across the table and took both of her hands in his, stifling her determination to tell him about his aunt's will. "Then don't go. Stay here with me. I'll call Charlie Conway and tell him to get another photographer. I like you, Orion, and I don't want you to leave, either."

"Christian, there's nothing I would like better, but I can't do that. I gave my word, and as much as I want to stay, that's how much I want to cover this story. Please understand. Photography is part of my life. I can't just . . . just throw it in on a whim." At the look on Christian's face, she added hastily, "Not that this is a whim, it's just that I have to tell . . ." Not knowing what else to say, she sat miserably in her chair.

"Believe it or not, I understand. There will be other days and other nights," he said meaningfully.

Sam forced a chilling note into her tone when she replied, "Mr. Delaney, I think I should tell you that I do not sleep around, nor would I be any good at one-night stands. I have a tendency to lock into situations. Now, if you would like to revise that last statement of yours to read, 'there will be other days and other evenings,' I can go away on this assignment with a clear head and have something to look forward to on my return. I do like you and I want to see you again, but I also don't want you to get the wrong idea or later say that I misled you. That's why I want you to know..."

"I do know. And you could never mislead me, Orion." Was she mistaken, or was his face registering shocked disbelief at her words? Had she really said those things aloud? Evidently. Up front. Always be up front with everyone, Gemini had said. People always respected honesty and forthrightness. Sure they did, Sam thought cynically. *I think you blew it that time, Gemini.*

"I have to leave now," Sam said, looking at the circlet on her wrist. "But before I do..."

"I'll drive you to the airport. I can't let you take a taxi. What would you think of me?"

Exasperated, Sam tossed her napkin onto the table. Would this man never let her speak? If she wanted to make her plane on time, she'd have to give it up as hopeless. The first thing she would do on her return would be to sit him down and tell it like it was. A minuscule twinge of guilt nipped her conscience. Had she really done her best to tell him, or was this assignment more important than the truth? "It's not necessary to take me to the airport, but I would like it, if you're serious," she was astonished to hear herself say in a smooth voice.

"Orion, you have no idea just how serious I am. This probably sounds a little corny, but I enjoyed that little speech of yours a minute ago. I hope we do have many days and evenings together. Let's pick up your duffel and get out of here."

Sam walked on air out to the yellow sports car and was in seventh heaven all the way to the airport. At least it was seventh heaven as long as she didn't allow herself to think about what a coward she was for not revealing to Christian that she was the Sam Blakely he was seeking—seeking to wring his neck, she reminded herself. It was all a mistake; she was certain of it. As soon as that doddering old lawyer looked into the matter, everything would straighten itself out. Gemini couldn't have left her anything besides the two cats. It was unthinkable. All Gemini had ever said was that the two cats were going to be Sam's responsibility, and Samantha had assumed that taking the cats would somehow repay Gemini for the countless kindnesses the old woman had shown her. Besides, this was no time to be revealing anything to the publisher and president of the magazine that was giving her the first big break at becoming a successful photojournalist. She couldn't take the chance of having Christian become so angry that he took the brush fire assignment away from her.

To Sam's surprise, instead of dropping her off at the terminal, Christian parked his car and escorted her to the ticket counter. Ramon Gill was standing just beyond the ticket line, sporting his *Daylight* press badge so she would recognize him. Ramon's Latin eyes flicked over her appraisingly. "So, you're Orion. Somehow, I wasn't expecting someone as pretty as you."

Sam's trigger had been pulled, and she almost bristled with a stinging retort about how being a female photographer didn't necessarily mean you had to look like a dragon. But she thought better of it. If she was to work successfully with Ramon Gill, that would mean they had to be on good terms. Instead of giving him a sharp retort, she smiled a coy thanks for his compliment.

"Ramon, have you met our president? Mr. Christian Delaney."

Gill's eyebrows raised in surprise. "Yeah, I've heard there was somebody new in the front office. How do you do, Mr. Delaney? I've followed your work on the foreign market, and as a journalist, I appreciate it. You've gotten our reporters into some newsfronts where even *Time* magazine was unwelcome."

"I did my best," Christian answered, shaking Ramon's hand firmly. "Listen, why don't you go and grab a cup of coffee? There's still time before the takeoff. Orion and I have a few things to discuss.''

"Yeah, sure," Ramon agreed affably. "Say, Orion, want me to take your duffel with me? It's good to see a woman who can pack sensibly. I was sort of worried that you'd come with fifty-nine suitcases and that we'd have to wait all night for the baggage. I always travel with carry-on bags myself."

Sam handed Ramon her duffel. "I appreciate it." As Ramon reached for her camera and gadget bag, Sam stepped backward. "These stay with me, always."

"Sure." Gill shrugged. "I know all about it. I ought to. I've been working with you camera people long enough. The camera never leaves your side, right?"

"Right."

"Okay. See you at the boarding gate." With a nod to Christian, Ramon hefted his own duffel plus Sam's and headed for the coffee shop.

"You handled that very well." Christian smiled down at her. "I could see that you were just ripping to straighten out Ramon's thinking about female photographers. Restraint and discretion are the better part of valor.''

Sam laughed. ''Am I that transparent?''

Christian looked down into her upturned face, a long, penetrating look that seemed to steal her breath away. ''Come on,'' he prodded. ''You're going to get a proper send-off.''

''And what is that?''

''A beer in the V.I.P. lounge and then a very sound kiss just before you board.''

All the while they conversed over their beers in the softly lit V.I.P. lounge, Sam's thoughts were focused ahead on the kiss he promised her just before she boarded the plane. The conversation was lighthearted and she joined Christian in some teasing banter, but all the while her eyes drank in the familiar planes of his face, the tiny cleft in his chin, the lines around his eyes that said he had spent a good deal of time in a hot, sunny climate, the slight salting of gray near his temples, and, most of all, the lights that glowed from the depths of his silvery-gray eyes.

She liked the way the corners of his mouth lifted when he smiled. The slight tilt at the end of his nose hinted at his Irish heritage. His heavy, almost unruly, brows added a sternness to his features that was waylaid by the humor in his smile. Fleetingly, she wondered if anyone, even a great artist, could capture this man's vitality and masculinity on canvas. Now, to her discerning eye, she realized how flat and inaccurate the portrait in her spare bedroom really was. It was the image of this man, not the great personality and charm he exuded.

Christian glanced at his watch. "I'd better get you down to the gate now, or I'll just sweep you up and refuse to let you leave me. You're very beautiful, you know. And I like the way your eyes flash when you laugh. You have a very nice laugh, Orion, and I intend to hear it often when you get back from your forest fire." His tone was deep and husky; the expression in his eyes excited her.

They ran, hand in hand, toward the gate where her plane was waiting and had just arrived when the flight was announced over the public address system. Sam's heart beat like a trip-hammer at the thought of his promised kiss. She wanted that kiss, needed it, and shamelessly knew that she was anticipating it.

Her hand shook slightly as she handed her boarding pass to the flight attendant. Suddenly, Christian had wrapped his arms around her and drew her close into his embrace. For a long moment he gazed down into her eyes before he lowered his head and pressed his lips to her mouth.

The touch was light, fleeting, teasing. His strong arms held her, refusing to allow her to escape. Again, he looked down into her eyes, an expression of surprise glowing in the depths of his own. The room seemed to spin; all sound was muted; only the drumbeat of her heart sounded in her ears. And when again his head lowered to hers, his mouth possessed hers, demanding an answering response, giving a promise of things to come.

"Sir. Sir!" the flight attendant insisted. "Sir, you are hampering the other passengers from boarding the plane. Sir!"

Reluctantly, Christian released Sam. Bewilderment and surprise were struck on his features. "Orion..."

"Please, sir, you are blocking traffic!"

"Off you go, Orion. I'll be waiting," he murmured huskily. "Get going before I steal you away," he added gruffly.

In a trance, Samantha hurried down the corridor to the plane. Dazedly, she found her seat beside Ramon and fastened her seatbelt. Her lips were still tingling with the touch of Christian's kiss. Her body felt the hot imprint of where his arms had held her. Shaken, she pushed her camera bag beneath the seat and tried to control her rising emotions. She was almost looking forward to the long flight to California. She needed time. Time to think.

Ramon stirred beside her. "That was quite a little scene you and Delaney performed out there. And, by the way, it's nice to know there are still some girls who can blush."

Chapter Three

Tired, giddy with success, Sam stopped dead in her tracks in the middle of the airport parking lot and stared at her companion, Ramon Gill. A surge of laughter overcame her, and she wiped tears away with the back of a grimy hand. "You should only see what you look like! I swear, Ramon, there's a decided odor of singed hair and charcoal wafting this way."

"Ha!" Ramon snapped. "They'll never place you on the ten best-dressed list. And that isn't exactly Arpege clinging to you. I'd sell my soul for a shower and a fresh change of clothes right now. The least you could have done was to make a later flight reservation so we could have showered. You in a hurry or something?'' he asked, unlocking the door of his Corvette.

"Or something.'' Samantha grinned. "If I never smell smoke again, I'll be just as happy.'' Jackknifing herself into the Corvette, she settled herself and leaned back against the seat.

"That's it, sleep,'' Ramon chided as he slipped the key into the ignition. "You women are all alike. Here I am, wounded in battle and just as exhausted as you, and yet I have to drive. Where to, lady? And it better not be Maryland.''

Sam smiled. "Wounded, are you? Since when do they give the Purple Heart for singed eyebrows?''

Ramon returned her smile. They had formed a mutual appreciation for one another during the assignment of following the forest fire. Together, they had discovered that they were both unyielding when it came to covering the news story to the best of their ability. Instinctively, they had assisted one another, falling into an easy rapport. Ramon put the words on the paper, and Orion's photographs brought them to life.

"I repeat, Orion, where to?" he asked as he paid the parking fee at the booth near the edge of the lot. "In other words, where do you live?"

Sam was instantly awake, her mind racing. She had forgotten. How could she go back to her apartment? Christian Delaney said he was hiring private detectives to track down the "gigolo" who had befriended his Aunt Gemini. If she went back to the brownstone before she could make her explanations to Christian, she would be spotted and then the fur would fly. She was too tired for confrontations, for explanations, and there was no way she could face Christian at the moment. For now, at least, evasion would be the best tactic. And it might continue to be until she could straighten out this mess. With any luck at all, the ancient lawyer would have discovered his error by now concerning the fifty-one percent of the stock being left in her name.

Samantha drew a deep breath and exhaled slowly. "Actually, Ramon," she said airily, "I was thinking that perhaps you could drop me off at the airport Holiday Inn. It won't be out of your way. I'm just too tired to go back to my apartment and wait for the water to get hot and for the heat to come on. All I want is a shower and sleep. Just drop me off." Before Ramon could answer, Sam had taken her duffel bag from the back seat and had her camera slung over her shoulder.

Ramon glanced at his companion suspiciously. "If Holiday Inns are your thing, it's okay with me. I'm going to stop by the magazine. Do you have any messages to deliver?"

"I'll call Charlie after I take a shower and brush my teeth. Do you think it's possible to have cinders and soot in your teeth?"

"Anything is possible," Ramon muttered as he swung the Corvette down the ramp to pull alongside the entrance to the Holiday Inn.

"Thanks for the ride, Ramon." Sam grinned at the journalist's second suspicious look and waited on the curb for the sports car to swing onto Jefferson Davis Highway. The second the fast-moving car was out of sight, Sam hefted the duffel over her shoulder and headed for the Crystal Underground Shopping Center. An hour later she was laden with two burgeoning shopping bags, compliments of her American Express and Visa cards. She had to have clothes, and since she had decided not to go back to her apartment for the time being, she had no other choice but to buy new clothing from the skin out.

The motel room's door double-locked and the chain in place, Sam turned the shower on full blast and stripped down. She stood under the needle-sharp spray, letting the tiny beads of water wash away the top layer of soot and grime that had worked their way through her clothes. She lathered her silky skin twice and managed to shampoo her hair at the same time. What seemed like forever later to her, she stepped from the cascading water and wrapped herself in the skimpy motel towels.

First things first. How much had she charged with her plastic money? Recklessly, she rummaged through the shopping bags until she had a neat pile of receipts in her hand. Mentally, she tallied them up and gulped. Cash—how much cash did she have? With one eye closed to ward off disappointment, she peered at the thin sheaf of bills in her wallet. A grand total of sixty-three dollars. Darn, why did she feel like such a criminal? She hadn't done anything except be nice to an old lady of whom she had genuinely been fond. Another one-eyed look in her checkbook told her she wouldn't be able to camp out in a motel much longer, not at forty-two dollars a day plus food. She would have to face Christian Delaney, and soon.

Sam returned both the checkbook and credit slips to her purse. She popped a crystal mint into her mouth and dialed the main number at the magazine. The switchboard operator put her on hold. Sam leaned back against the propped-up pillows and was instantly asleep, the squawking phone in her hand.

Sam awoke refreshed, the alarm beeping on her digital watch, at eight a.m. She vaguely remembered waking up once during the night to total darkness and also vaguely remembered hanging up the phone. She opened the drapes and peered out at the tall building on top of the Crystal Underground from her fourth-floor room. It was difficult to tell exactly what kind of day it was. It looked cold, and here she was with nothing more than a heavy sweater purchased at the shopping center. She had to get her own clothes or she would freeze to death.

She showered, taking her time, and then called down for room service and was informed that all meals were served on disposable plates with plastic implements. She had time for a leisurely breakfast and the ride into the city. The first day back after an assignment was always a slow day to catch up. It was either a congratulation or gripe-and-complaint day. Either way, it was still slow.

A drab gray light filtered through the window at her cubbyhole office at *Daylight Magazine* and directed Sam's attention to a small stack of mail which rested on her desk.

Before she could begin to open the vari-sized envelopes, Charlie Conway slouched into the office. "You did a good job, kid. The lighting on those pics is some of the best I've ever seen. Just in case you're interested, the front office asked for a complete set of photos. I expect you'll get some praise from on high. You did a good job, and Ramon had only good things to say about the way you work, and coming from him, that's the best."

Sam smiled happily. "Ramon actually said that?"

Charlie rolled his cigar around in his mouth a couple of times and grinned. "Actually, what he said was you were okay but weird, and you had this thing about motels. Oh, yeah, he said you forgot where you lived."

Sam flushed and then laughed. "I was so tired, Charlie, and what with the jet lag, I just didn't have the stamina to go all the way back into town. I tried calling you, but the girl put me on hold and I fell asleep and didn't wake up till this morning."

"You're forgiven. I'll forgive anything you do if you keep giving me pics like the ones of the fire. You got a lunch date? I'd like to hear about the fire."

"No, I don't have a lunch date, but I have to run a few errands. I can stop by your office later if you want and we could have a cup of coffee and talk about it, unless you have another assignment for me."

"You're on call. It's a date, then. Any time this afternoon is okay; the rag has been put to bed."

"Didn't Ramon fill you in?" Sam asked inquisitively.

"Ramon told me to read about it in the magazine. He's like a superstitious old gypsy. He'll talk my ear off once the rag hits the street, but not one second before."

Sam watched the old editor as he exited the office, an ominous, billowing cloud of foul gray smoke in his wake. She fanned furiously at the air and was startled to see Christian Delaney standing in the doorway. "Welcome back, Orion." He smiled from ear to ear.

Sam felt her heart begin to thud. It seemed to have some kind of bongo rhythm all its own as she stared at the handsome man in the doorway. "Th-thank you. It's good to be back." She waited, uncertain if she should get up and hold out her hand, or if she should stay seated behind the rough, scarred desk. You didn't shake hands with a man you kissed, not if you kissed him the way she had, anyway. Throwing caution to the winds and ignoring her fast-beating heart, she rose and walked over to the publisher. She grinned and said, "Come in, said the spider to the fly." Christian Delaney needed no second urging.

"The question is: Who's the spider and who's the fly?" He grinned back as he drew her to him.

"Hmm, does it matter?" Sam murmured as she nuzzled her head against his chest.

"Not to me, it doesn't," Christian said huskily as his mouth met hers. The kiss was butterfly soft, yet demanding in its intensity.

Sam moved slightly and stared deeply into Christian's eyes. "I liked that. Kiss me again," she said boldly.

They were both shaking when Christian released her and held her away from him at arm's length. Sam stared back, knowing her feelings were revealed in her shaky gaze. She swallowed hard. She couldn't have uttered a word if her life depended on it. Apparently, Christian felt the same way, for he kissed her lightly on the cheek and opened the door. "Dinner," he said gruffly. "After work, around six." Sam nodded.

"How...how di-did you like the pictures?" Sam blurted. Suddenly, she couldn't bear for him to leave her office. From this moment on, she knew she was going to love this small, confining space with a passion unequaled.

"Pictures? What pictures? Oh, those pictures! Good, very good. I liked them." He turned, his face serious, the silvery-gray eyes hooded. "You're some kind of woman, Orion! Did anyone ever tell you that?"

Sam grinned. It was okay for him to leave now. "Only my dad, and I'm not sure that counts."

"Let's keep it that way," Christian said over his shoulder as he strode briskly down the corridor.

A silly look on her face, Sam slumped in the creaking swivel chair. It was a beautiful cubbyhole, and it smelled just as beautiful as she sniffed at the faint, almost elusive, scent of the publisher's cologne. She had to find out what it was and buy a gallon of it. She would spritz it all around. "I'm in love!" she chortled happily. Her happiness was short-lived when she remembered how she was duping Gemini's nephew. She had to tell him. Tonight, she would tell him, after dinner, when he took her home.

Don't think about that now. Why not? her mind questioned. *There isn't anything else to do.* "Yes, there is," she said aloud. "I didn't open my mail." Quickly, she sifted through the mail and sorted it into piles. Circulars, sale flyers from various department stores, bills, two letters from college friends who insisted on keeping in touch, and a legal-looking envelope from the Women's Bank. Her bank. She slit open the envelope and withdrew a pale green check attached to a letter. One short paragraph that said Sam Blakely was due the enclosed third-quarter dividend check from the Delaney stocks.

Beyond realizing that the amount was in six figures, she couldn't comprehend the actual sum. She had no basis for comprehending money in such large amounts. Sam lowered her eyes at the slip of paper she was holding. She gagged and the check fluttered and fell to the floor. Transfixed, unable to move, her eyes followed the square of paper. She gagged again and covered her mouth with both her hands. It couldn't be! There was a dreadful mistake! There just wasn't that much money in the whole world! And they sent it in the mail, she thought in horror. Oh, God! Oh, God, what was she going to do? Pick it up, of course. You didn't leave $667,395.42 laying on the floor. Gingerly, she picked up the check and stared at it again. Did one fold a check for this amount? Was it one of those that you did not fold, spindle, or mutilate? Quickly, she opened her top desk drawer and dropped the check onto a pile of blank paper. She slammed the drawer closed with shaking hands and held it in place. Slowly, she inched the drawer open a fraction. It was still there. Oh, God, it was still there! She would give it back to

Christian tonight when she told him who she was. He would know what to do with it. That's what she would do.

Gemini, how could you do this to me? she wailed silently. *He's never going to understand. I can feel it.* Blind panic covered her like a mantle and then coursed through her veins, leaving her weak-kneed and trembling. There had to be a way out of this; she just had to find it. She would put herself in Christian Delaney's place and try to react the way he would. Now, let's see, first she would explain and then hand him the check. He would say something magnanimous like, "Why thank you, Ms. Blakely. There aren't too many people in the world who would return a check for $667,395.42. Believe me, I understand perfectly why you're returning it. You're returning it because it's a mere drop in the bucket compared to what you would get from our relationship if we married. Even the lowliest copy runner at the magazine knows I'm the heir to the Delaney publishing fortune. When you compare $667,395.42 to a fortune, it doesn't take much imagination to know which one you'll pick." A squeal of pure agony escaped her tight lips. She *couldn't* tell him! She *had* to tell him! She would compromise. She would tell him later, much later. For now, she wanted more time with him, more time to feel his lips and arms around her, so when she was in the dark days to come, she would at least have memories. Gemini had lived on her memories for the last forty years. She would have memories and $667,395.42. And this was just the third quarter. If she were to take that amount and multiply it times four, she would have... Oh, God! She had to give it back. Perhaps what she should do was to send it anonymously to the bank president. She was a woman; she'd understand.

An unseen devil perched itself on Sam's shoulder and whispered, "It's yours; Gemini saw to it. It's all legal. You don't really have to give it back. Why not take a 'wait and see' attitude? If Delaney finds out who you are, see how he handles it before you return the money. You could find yourself out in the cold without a job, an apartment. That dividend check will buy a lot of warmth."

"Not the kind of warmth I'm looking for," Sam snarled at the invisible devil. "I won't do it. I'm giving it back!"

A copy boy stuck his head in the door and yelled, "Catch!" And he tossed her a heavy manila envelope. "Charlie wants you to go over Ramon Gill's story and space the pics."

Sam nodded and flipped open the envelope. Thank heaven for work. Thank heaven for anything that would take her mind off the slip of paper in her desk drawer.

Working industriously for the next several hours, Sam managed to finish up her work a few minutes before six. Time for a quick spruce-up and a dab of fresh makeup and she would be ready to meet Christian for dinner. Her heart fluttered wildly at the thought and then thumped heavily in her chest. What was she going to do with the check? She couldn't carry it with her; you just didn't carry that kind of check around. She couldn't leave it in the office drawer. The safe. She would ask Charlie Conway to put it in his safe. Too late; he was gone. Vaguely, she remembered smelling his cigar as he walked by the office and said something about seeing her in the morning. Now what was she going to do? The first thing she should do was put the green slip in another envelope. *Hide it!* her mind screamed. *Where?* She answered herself. The only place left—Christian Delaney's safe. What better place. She would seal it, scribble her name on the envelope, and forget about it. Ha! How did a person who had $889.88 to her name forget about a small green piece of paper bearing her name and the sum of $667,395.42. One didn't forget; what one did was ignore it. Immediately, she felt better and she felt positively light-headed once the check was safe inside a manila envelope. Carefully, she sealed the metal hook beneath three layers of Scotch tape. Her hands were trembling so badly she tangled the tape around her fingers and finally ended up pulling the sticky tape apart with her teeth. The matter tended to, she literally fell into the swivel chair and collapsed. She wasn't meant to have money, not if it did this to her. Disgust washed through her as she stared at the square envelope in front of her. Disgust gave way to pity for herself as she continued to stare at the fateful envelope. *Gemini, you shouldn't have done this. Whatever possessed you to do such a thing?* Finding no answers, Sam mentally affixed an invisible ramrod to her spine and stood up. Before she could think twice, she picked up the envelope and marched down the hall to Christian Delaney's office. The door stood open and she knocked lightly before entering.

The scene was an exact replica of the first time played out in the publisher's office. The handsome publisher stood with his back to her, shouting into the phone. Sam blanched at the words and dropped the manila square she was holding. She didn't want to listen, didn't want to hear more ways the man was going to kill her. She should leave, run as fast as her slim legs would carry her, but she couldn't. Not yet. She would punish herself and listen.

The words were ice cold and the harshest she had ever heard. "It's been seven days! What do you mean you have one lead and you aren't even sure of that? Fine, if money is your problem, then put more men on the case. I told you before I didn't care what it costs. Find Sam Blakely! Did you check with the postman? His mail was being held at the post office and was picked up today. Right, it was picked up today! Do you want to know why it was picked up today? I'll tell you why!'' Christian Delaney thundered into the phone. "The dividend checks went out in the mail this week for the third quarter. Right now, this minute, he's probably winging his way to the Mediterranean intent on bilking some other old lady. Check the airlines. Now that that weasel has money to burn, he's apt to go first class. Gigolos do that. What do you mean, how do I know that? I just know. What about the Division of Motor Vehicles? He doesn't own a car. It figures. Try the rental agencies. I understand you can rent a Mercedes for a very small down payment. My aunt would never ride in anything but a Mercedes or a Checker cab. I'm certain you never thought of that,'' Christian said sarcastically.

Christian turned and motioned for Sam to sit down. He rolled his eyes in apology and again turned to face the panoramic view of the nation's Capitol. "I can't wait to hear your lead. Let's have it. A man named Sam Blakely. What street? Spell it; Kilbourne Place, off Mount Pleasant Avenue. Do you have a number? Amazing! Second floor, number 1755. I have it. You're right I'm going up there, and right now. When was he seen last? Of course I'm edgy. And I'll stay edgy until he's behind bars or I have my hands around his neck. I'll call you later.''

Sam's brain was working double time and her fingers were fidgeting with the shoulder strap of her heavy canvas bag. When Christian turned to her and smiled, her heart melted and she wanted to leap up and throw her arms around him. He must have felt the same way, because he crooked his finger slightly, beckoning her to him. She fell into his arms and sighed deeply. Gently, Christian stroked her soft curls and held her close. ''If I kiss you now,'' he whispered huskily, ''we'll never get around to dinner.''

Sam moved slightly from his embrace and smiled. ''Charlie Conway is gone and I want to put this in the safe. Will you do it for me?''

Christian reached for the envelope and turned it over, looking at both sides. "You didn't put your name on it." Not waiting for her to answer, he picked up a black grease pencil and scrawled "Orion" across the front. "It doesn't feel as though there's anything in it."

Sam forced another weak smile and remained silent.

Christian twirled the dial on the wall safe and then deposited the envelope. Locking the safe, he smacked his hands together. "Okay, let's get out of this place. I have a stop to make before we go to dinner. I hope you don't mind, but it really can't wait. I'm sure you heard my end of the conversation, so you know what's been going on. By God, the nerve of that weasel!"

"What . . . what weasel?" Sam gulped.

"The weasel who duped my Aunt Gemini and the weasel we're on our way to see. That weasel!"

"Oh," Sam said inanely, "that weasel."

"He's the one. When I'm finished with him, he'll never prey on another poor, unsuspecting old lady again."

"Is that wise?" Sam asked hesitantly. "What I mean is, you can get yourself into a lot of trouble taking this matter into your own hands. Besides, perhaps there's been a mistake..."

"If there's one thing I can't stand, it's deceit," Christian interrupted through clenched teeth. "I despise lies and trickery. I may have been born into money, but it's meant nothing to me. I receive a salary just like everyone else here at Delaney Enterprises. My parents saw to it that I worked my way through life. At the age of twelve I had two paper routes because I wanted a new bicycle. I worked summers.... What I've done, I've done myself. The money that's come to me through the family has barely been touched. I don't live the life of a playboy. As for the shares my poor misguided aunt left to that Sam Blakely, just let it suffice to say that I want it back. All of it. This has been a family-owned business, and as far as I'm concerned, it will always be. Fifty-one percent of the stock is the controlling interest. How can I ensure the growth of this company if the controlling stock is owned by a Sam Blakely? There's a lot at stake, and I intend to settle it—immediately!''

Sam was stunned. Why was he telling her this? Was this his way of making his threats known? Could it be he already suspected that she was Sam Blakely? Oh, if ever there was a time to bare her soul, this was it. Swallowing hard, she forced her tongue to working order and managed a garbled, "Christian, there's something I think...what I mean is, I'd like to talk to you..."

"Darling, remember what you were going to say. We've got to get moving. Tell me over dinner."

She knew she should have insisted. Allowing him to cut her off was too easy. Now was the time, before things went too far, before it was impossible to tell him, and then he would find out sooner or later and hate her for it. But it was not to be. Christian took her by the arm and led her out of the office.

As Christian drove along the unfamiliar streets, he turned to Samantha. "I left my driving glasses back at the office. Watch for Mount Pleasant Avenue. This is Seventeenth Street, isn't it?'' Sam craned her neck backward and managed a jerky nod. "It should be along about here. It's been years since I've been in this area. If the trolley tracks were still here, it would be a breeze. There's something about streetcar tracks that make me melancholy.''

"Turn left, Christian. There's Mount Pleasant Avenue,'' Sam said quietly. What had she been thinking of? She had actually been going to tell him. If she had, he never would have called her ''darling.'' She meant something to him. She was certain of it. And he certainly meant something to her; just how much, she was afraid to even measure. ''Kilbourne Place on your left. What number are you looking for?''

"End of the block, number 1755, second-floor apartment!''

Christian guided the car to the curb and sat for a moment. "I shouldn't have brought you with me. This doesn't look like the kind of neighborhood that's safe to walk around in after dark. I'm not even sure the car will still be here once we come out of the build-ing.''

Sam looked at the grimy brick building and winced. Venetian blinds that held years of dirt were hanging lopsidedly on the cracked windows. One window on the second floor was being propped open with a portable television set. A tattered blue curtain fluttered wildly. A sudden gust of wind came up, and dry leaves hurtled through the open window. What if some thug lived inside and he attacked them both?

"Lock your door, Orion, and hold on to my arm," Christian said, holding open the door for Sam.

Clutching Christian's muscular arm, Sam walked with him up the brick steps into a filthy hallway that reeked of years of stale food and other nauseating odors. Cautiously, they made their way to the top of the rickety steps with the aid of a fifteen-watt bulb that hung precariously from a frayed electrical wire.

Christian rapped loudly on the door and then stepped back, pulling Sam with him. No answer. He rapped again and kicked at the bottom of the door at the same time. "Yeah, whatcha want this time?" a whining voice demanded. Sam felt faint at the sight of the wizened old man who opened the door.

Christian stepped back another step and asked forcefully. "Is your name Sam Blakely?"

"And what if it is. My old mum gave me that name seventy-two years ago, and I'm still using it, so what business is it of yours?"

Christian ignored the question and asked another. "How long have you lived here?"

"As long as the cockroaches—and that's forever. Who are you, anyway?"

"Did you know Gemini Delaney?" Christian demanded in an angry tone.

"Don't know no Gemini anyone. Crazy name if you ask me. I ain't into that star stuff myself. Matter of fact, I just got out of the hospital today. Was in there for a whole month. I had pneumonia," the old man said proudly. "'Course, I was in the charity ward, but they took care of me just like everyone else, and they even called me Mr. Blakely. It's important for a man not to lose his identity. I was born Sam Blakely, and I'm gonna die Sam Blakely. Say, now, what you gonna pay me for answering all these questions? Listen, you ain't from one of them there TV shows, are you—you know, the hidden camera one?''

"No," Christian said disgustedly. "Look, I'm sorry to have bothered you. Here," he said, handing the old man a twenty-dollar bill. "Buy yourself a good steak and some vegetables and see to it that all the good they did for you in the hospital doesn't go to waste.''

"That's mighty nice of you, Mister. You sure you ain't from one of them TV shows and they're going to come here and take this money from me after they turn off the cameras?''

"I'm sure," Christian said over his shoulder as he guided Sam down the dim stairway. "Don't touch anything, Orion.''

Outside in the fresh air Sam gulped and swallowed hard. Poor Christian. She had to tell him; she couldn't allow him to keep searching like this. He looked so defeated.

Inside the car with the doors locked, Christian drove through Rock Creek Park. He was silent for so long Sam began to feel apprehensive. She should say something to break his mood. She should tell him now before this charade went much further.

"Orion, I'm sorry. This was a beastly thing to subject you to. All I can do is apologize. This business with my aunt has me caught up in a whirlwind. No more unpleasantries. I've been looking forward to this evening since you left for California. This is our evening and I don't want anything to spoil it."

The husky, intimate tone of his voice sent tingles up her spine. She felt herself drawn to him, losing herself in him. When he looked at her that way, with a crinkle of a smile in the corners of his eyes, she was reduced to Silly Putty. All reason escaped her; all determination to confess her true identity evaporated. To keep herself from melting beneath his silver gaze, she struggled to find conversation. "Is anyone at the magazine taking up a collection or planning a party of some sort for Ramon Gill? He's getting married next month," she blurted.

"No. I didn't know. I'll speak to Charlie about having a luncheon or something. Gill has been with the magazine for a long time. It's the least we can do. You're a romantic, are you?"

"All women are romantics." Sam grinned in the darkness. "Are you a romantic, Christian?" she teased.

"Of the first order. But if you tell anyone, I'll deny it. How would it look to my staff if they found out I was all mush inside?"

Sam laughed and the tension was relieved. They were both relaxed now, with a long evening ahead of them. She would tell him tomorrow that the Sam Blakely he was seeking was right here—under his nose. Right now, she needed this man who claimed he was a romantic. She needed to feel him beside her, needed his comforting words, and, at the same time, perhaps she could give him something in return. *I can't fall in love with him; I just can't.* A tiny, niggling voice warned that it was too late. She was already in love with Christian Delaney.

Christian had made reservations at a marvelous German restaurant in downtown Washington. Beer was served in lagers, and hearty pork sausages and cabbage were the main fare. All through dinner, Tyrolean musicians played their wind instruments and strolled among the tables. Samantha was mesmerized. It was immediately apparent that Christian was a familiar patron from the way he was greeted by the waiters and maître d'. The service was impeccable and the atmosphere conducive to quiet conversation. Throughout dinner, Christian kept up a cheerful banter, never once mentioning his search for one Sam Blakely. Time and again Samantha would find herself looking into his silvery-gray eyes and feeling as though she would drown in his warm, lingering looks. His gaze touched her face, her hair, her eyes, her mouth, and ignited a flurry of strange yearnings and excitement that she had never known. Reaching across the table, he touched her hand, holding it, fondling it, possessing it, as though he would never let her go.

Sam wished that dinner would never end. She preened in his attention, became breathless under his sultry glances and in the promise that was in his eyes.

Christian was just suggesting a ride along the Potomac when the pager he wore on his belt beeped insistently. His tone was full of disappointment when he excused himself to phone the office.

Sam watched his retreating back as he made his way to the phones. Suddenly, as though coming out of a dream, she began to panic. The evening was almost over! Christian would be wanting to take her home! It was hopeless. She would not lie to him or, at best, evade the truth again! She would face his rage and fury and tell him who she was. She would pray he would understand. She respected him too much to deceive him any longer. And, heaven help her, she loved him.

As she was pondering her problem and mourning over the fact that she would lose both the man she loved and the job she wanted in one stroke, he reappeared at the table. "Penny for your thoughts. Orion, something's come up at the office. I've got to go back there. It's an important break in the Mideast story. It couldn't come at a worse time!"

"Time and news wait for no man, Christian," Sam murmured regretfully, secretly relieved that once again the decision to confess all was taken from her hands.

"Come on, I'll get you home before I go back to the office," he said as he signed the check.

"You don't have to worry about me. I can take a cab home. It's all right, really." She had to tell him, but she needed his undivided attention, and this was not the time, nor the place. Or was this line of thinking another indication of her cowardice? she wondered, disgusted with herself.

"No, it's not all right. I'll take you home and then I'll go to the office," he insisted as he took her arm and led her out of the restaurant.

As they waited for the attendant to bring his car around to the front, Samantha became rigid. "This is really silly, Christian. I can take a cab right from here to my doorstep. Really. I'll be fine."

"If you're certain," Christian compromised. "Tell you what, I'll leave my car here and send for it in the morning. I'll ride in the taxi with you as far as the magazine, and I'll make sure the driver gets you home safely."

Christian climbed into the cab beside her. "I'll make this up to you, I promise—as soon as possible."

Samantha smiled reassuringly. "I don't mind, not really. There's always a next time."

Christian pulled Sam into his arms. "There's no time like the present," he whispered against her ear. And when his mouth came crashing down on hers, she felt the earth move beneath her feet. It was a long, lingering kiss, a kiss that dreams were made of. It was a kiss that held promises and soft words. Words like love, and eternity....

Breathlessly, she pulled out of his embrace and leaned her cheek against his shoulder. "God, I hate to leave you. I could hold you like this forever. I've never felt this..."

"Sh!" She silenced him by pressing her finger to his lips. The panic was rising in her breast again. She couldn't let him declare his feelings for her until she confessed her relationship with his aunt. To do otherwise would be unfair, and he would hate her for it.

Chapter Four

Sam looked at her wrist for the third time in less than five minutes. She had to do it. She had to tell Christian Delaney that she was the Sam Blakely in question. He had to understand. And if he didn't, she would have to work double time to make him aware that she had nothing to do with Gemini's bequest, that she had been completely in the dark until the day the letter arrived from the lawyer.

A quick look in her tiny pocket mirror told her her face was on straight; nothing was smudged. She was glad now that she had chosen the raspberry silk dress and Halston perfume. She looked her best, and right now that feeling was paramount. Would Christian understand? Finding no answers to her tormenting questions, Sam took a deep breath and marched down the long, narrow hallway to the publisher's office. Blunt. She would tell him straight out and not mince words. Up front. No lies, no deceit. She would say it like it was and take whatever was coming to her.

Sam moistened dry lips and tapped quietly on the heavy door.

"Come in."

Sam's eyes closed momentarily and then she squared her shoulders. She was Daniel going into the lion's den. No, she was Samantha Blakely going into...

"Orion! What a pleasant surprise, and one with which I would like to start every day." How husky his voice was. How sensual his voice was. Yes, he was handsome. He was coming around the desk, ready to take her into his arms. He would kiss her and then she would tell him. No, she had to tell him first. She moved slightly out of his reach and then turned to stare at him for a brief second.

"There's something I have to talk to you about, Christian. It really can't wait another moment." Why was her voice cracking like this? *Because I care,* she answered herself.

"You sound so serious, Orion," Christian said in mock severity.

"I am serious, very serious. I tried to tell you several times, and you would always interrupt me, and then I finally lost my nerve and took the easy way out. I don't want you to do that again until I tell you what I have to... to... to say to you."

Christian's tone, as well as his expression, was both amused and indulgent. "Orion, you have my undivided attention. You may proceed. Look, I'm going to sit down so I won't tower over you."

Sam jammed her hands into the side pockets of the colorful dress so the publisher couldn't see how they were trembling. She took a deep breath and squared her shoulders. "Christian, I know that you will understand what I'm going to say because you are a man of...of...compassion. I know that you will understand that I tried on several occasions to tell you, but...what I mean is...you may at first think I was trying to...but...I wasn't...I am Sam Blakely," she finished lamely.

Christian Delaney neither moved nor spoke.

Sam rushed on. "I'm that...that dastardly person who owns fifty-one percent of this...this company. I didn't know until I got the letter from the lawyer! Say something! Please, you can't blame me! I didn't know! I don't want the fifty-one percent! I tried to tell you in the restaurant before I left for the West Coast, but you kept interrupting me. I wanted to tell you when I got back, but...I didn't mean to deceive you. It was just that things got out of hand and... and..."

Silvery-gray eyes stared at her and through her. How cold and dead they looked. There was no need for words on the publisher's part. His eyes said it all. As far as he was concerned, she, Sam Blakely, ceased to exist.

"It's not the way it seems, and I did try to explain, but you kept interrupting me," Sam said in a shaky voice. "You must believe me! I don't want this magazine or your aunt's money! I don't know why she did what she did. I'm telling you the truth. Why won't you believe me? Please," she pleaded, "don't look at me that way. I thought—I hoped—that you would be fair and understand." What was the use? He was listening to her, but he didn't hear a thing she said. It was over. She turned to leave, her legs like fresh Jell-O, barely holding her erect.

Christian's words, when they finally came, shocked her. "You'll never see a penny of my aunt's money. I'll fight you in every court in the land. Liars make poor showings in a courtroom. So be prepared."

Sam's shoulders drooped. She wasn't a liar. She wasn't. She had tried to tell him. She had wanted to tell him from the very beginning. And now, because of her willy-nilly procrastination, it was all over between the two of them. How he must hate her. Scalding tears burned her eyes as she closed the door softly behind her. How final, how terminal the small sound was. You closed a door and part of your life was left behind.

Shoulders slumped, feet dragging, Samantha faced the long, seemingly endless corridor back to her office. Her heart was choked in her throat and the world around her seemed dark and without life. Suddenly, someone was holding her arm, shaking it.

"Orion, Orion, have you heard what's going on?" It was Ramon, and from the look of him, he was excited.

Samantha dragged herself back into the world of the living. Sudden sounds of clacking typewriters bounced into her awareness. Noise and confusion made her blink. What was going on? From the look of things, something important. Efficient secretaries were ripping papers from their machines with the speed of sound. Sam glanced around for Charlie Conway, but he was nowhere in sight. Milling reporters huddled into groups, talking excitedly.

"C'mon, Orion, get with it! Haven't you heard? Guess not. Word just came in over the teletype. Break in the Mideast crisis," Ramon told her. "I think I'm going. Cross your fingers. I missed out when it happened, and Conway told me this would be my turn."

Instantly, comprehension dawned upon Samantha. This would be the story of the decade.

Ramon, seeing the fervor shining in her face, prodded, "Get in there, Orion. See if you can get Conway to let you come along. As long as you keep your mouth shut and click your shutter the way you did in California, you can tag along with me anywhere. If I were you, I'd go in there right now and plead your case."

Sam was stunned. It was the answer to her unasked prayer. She could go away and try to forget Christian Delaney. Lose herself in her work. When she got back, things might be straightened out. When he had time to think, Christian might decide... Oh, what was the use of tormenting herself like this? This, for now, just might be her answer. "Ramon, do you think Charlie will assign me?'' she asked, a note of desperation in her voice.

''No. But it will make you feel better. Lizzie is the one who's making the travel arrangements. I've already put in a good word for you. Everyone around here knows Lizzie runs this company.''

Sam looked puzzled. ''Lizzie is just a secretary.''

Ramon shrugged. ''So? She runs this company. Even Delaney does what she says. She's one of those people who's never wrong. And Delaney inherited her when he took over. Some say she was old man Delaney's mistress, and others say she was just a platonic friend. All I know is if Lizzie books a flight for you, you go. You'll learn, Orion.''

''Have you seen Charlie?''

''He's getting the roster ready. Go on, Orion. What have you got to lose?''

What did she have to lose? Nothing. Without Christian there was nothing left. This assignment could mean her emotional survival, and it was suddenly the most important thing in the world. She wanted to go, needed to go. "Ramon, are you sure? About my tagging along with you, I mean."

"Orion, you make me look good. I'm no fool. I saw your pics, and with my story that makes us a winning team. And"—he grinned, lasciviously—"you aren't half-bad to look at, either."

"Gee, thanks."

"Your turn." The journalist grinned.

"Well, you aren't half-bad yourself. I like the way you dead-dog a story. Of course, that Latin charm goes a long way with the ladies, and they're the ones who spill to you."

"It's the teeth, Orion. They flash like a beacon in the night. Gets them right here," he said, pounding his chest. "Get going before Conway thinks you aren't interested."

Sam inched her way between the milling journalists and photographers and finally made it to Charlie Conway's office with one bruised elbow and a skinned shin. Cautiously, she opened the door a crack and then walked in hesitantly. "Charlie...oh, Charlie! I want to go!" she said adamantly.

"So does everyone on the magazine. I want to go myself. Heck, I'd drop all of this in a minute, but they tell me I'm too old. How do you like that? I'm too old! Seasoned, maybe, but old—never! Those young pups out there, think they know everything. I'll let you know, Orion, at the same time everyone else knows. If it's any consolation to you, Gill was in here three times pleading your case. You're late," he snapped.

"I just got here. I really want to go, Charlie."

"Chcck it out with Lizzie," Charlie said, relighting his stubby cigar.

"Does she really run this magazine?" Sam asked curiously.

"I think so. She sure tells me what to do. This roster is a farce. The real story is who she's making the travel arrangements for. It's a game we play around here. When the smoke clears, we match up our lists just to see how close I came to hers. It's a stupid way of doing business, but, she hasn't goofed once in all the years I've known her. Go on, see if she's got your name on the list.

Get out of here. Can't you see I have work to do?'' the old man said gruffly.

Sam watched Conway pick up a dart and throw it at a penciled likeness of Lizzie that was tacked to the door. "Ha! Right on the nose!'' Charlie chortled as the dart found its mark.

Lizzie was built like a dowager queen and that was how she reigned in the front reception area. Sam made her way to the marble foyer and stood staring at the woman behind the desk. Her pencil was flying over a sheaf of papers, making notes and canceling out other notes. She peered over the top of her glasses and picked out a pencil from her top knot of spiky gray curls.

"You got a problem, Orion, or do you just naturally stare at people?'' she asked in a gravelly voice.

"Both, I guess. Am I on your list, Lizzie?''

"Did Gill send you in here?''

Sam nodded. "I just found out you run this place. I thought Mr. Delaney was..."

"He is. I am. I'll get back to you. Run along now, I'm busy. Ah, by the way, did the dart hit my nose or my top lip?"

Sam watched in horror as the old lady whipped out a dart and aimed it at a faded newspaper clipping of Charlie Conway. Peals of scratchy laughter erupted from the receptionist as the dart found its mark.

Panic gripped Sam's stomach muscles. Had that been a look of pity in Lizzie's eyes when she posed her question? Or was she becoming paranoid about everything? What had she been asked? Whatever it was, the woman was obviously waiting for an answer. "Yes," Sam muttered weakly as she walked back toward Ramon.

"Well?" Ramon snapped, clutching at her arm.

"She said she would get back to me. I have a gut feeling I'm not going to go, so be prepared. The gods aren't looking on me too favorably right now," Sam said morosely.

They waited for over an hour before Christian Delaney made his appearance in the newsroom.

Lizzie and Charlie stood behind Christian, each holding a slip of paper. First Charlie handed the publisher his, and then Lizzie held hers out. Sam watched, holding her breath, as Christian compared both slips of paper. "It's a tie." His eyes narrowed as he scanned the list a second time. "I want to say, here and now, that I am the one who has final approval of this list, and there are one or two changes I think should be made." Sam's heart thudded, knowing what was coming.

"According to this, Orion is the only woman selected. It's too dangerous, Lizzie. Charlie, what about Mac Williams? Orion hasn't been in the Mideast. Take her off the list."

Sam's spirits fell to her shoes. How could he do this to her in front of a room full of people? Tears stung her eyes as the journalists and photographers dropped their eyes to avoid seeing her humiliation and hurt. This was a deliberate slap in the face, his way of getting back at her. How could he do this to her! How dare he!

Sam stared at Christian Delaney, hardly believing his words. How could he humiliate her this way? And then another feeling coursed through her—that alien feeling she had come to know so well. She was hurt, hurt to the core of her being. Did he really think she wasn't good enough to go with the others? Was he really denying her the chance to go along because she was a woman, or was he getting even with her because he hated her? Tears of self-pity flooded her eyes and she gulped back a threatened sob. Her shoulders squared imperceptibly. She couldn't let him know how she felt. She was a professional, and professionals didn't weep and wail when something wasn't to their liking. She had to put on a good face and make out the best she could. Maybe he thought he was fooling the others, but she knew why she wasn't being permitted to go.

The looks on the men's faces told her all she needed to know. She was on her own. You didn't cross the boss or ever tell him what to do. It was part of their code. Christian Delaney was the publisher and president. He was supposed to know what he was doing; that's why he was a boss. Ramon Gill shrugged and walked away, the others following.

Sam's throat constricted. She had to say something. How could she just walk back to her cubbyhole office without making a fight of it? She couldn't. Her voice, when she spoke, surprised her; it was even and calm, belying the turmoil she felt. "I think I'm good enough to go with the others. It saddens me that, as my employer, you feel I'm lacking in ability...and other things, as well. I know that..."

"Spare me, Orion, whatever philosophy you're about to spiel off." Sam was stunned at the cold, arrogant look of the man as he towered over her. He was so close she could smell the faint minty aroma of his breath. "My decision stands; you remain behind. You may own fifty-one percent of this magazine, but I am still president and publisher."

"It was a mistake. I don't really own the controlling interest," Sam said, a note of panic creeping into her voice.

A muscle twitched in Christian Delaney's cheek; and, if possible, his voice was even more chilling, his eyes more steely, his stance more arrogant when he spoke. "Oh, there's no mistake; you own the controlling interest, all right. Even if you owned ninety-nine and eight-tenths percent of the stock, you still wouldn't be permitted to go with the others. It's not safe; you'd hinder the others. Regardless of what you say or think, a woman is a woman, and all the men would feel responsible for you. Get it through that air head of yours—E.R.A. hasn't caught up over there. My orders stand. Now, get back to work before I decide to dock your pay."

Sam was mortified beyond words. She stared a moment at the publisher's retreating back and then ran to her office and slammed the door shut. Great choking sobs tore at her throat. Air head! He had called her an air head! He had added insult to injury. The slender shoulders shook with the intensity of her sobs. All of this was happening to her because of Gemini's generosity. Why couldn't he realize it was all a mistake? That fifty-one percent was going to make trouble for her in more ways than one. What hurt most of all was he didn't believe her; he sincerely believed that she had duped his aunt into leaving her the controlling interest in *Daylight Magazine*. He was so wrong. Why wouldn't he listen to her? Did he really hate her so much?

"I didn't do anything wrong," Sam whimpered to the empty office. "The only thing I'm guilty of is falling in love with him. I love him, I love him," she sobbed heartbrokenly. She sniffed and dabbed at her eyes and then blew her nose lustily. "I'll show him. I'll show him that I don't care about the assignment. I'll make him understand, somehow, that I don't want or need his aunt's legacy. If it takes me the rest of my life, I'll make him understand." It was a hopeless thought, and Sam knew it in her heart. Christian Delaney hated her. A chill washed over her when she remembered his steely eyes and his icy words.

One weary day after another passed. Sam's eyes hungered for a glimpse of the publisher as she went about the mundane chores that Charlie Conway assigned her.

Once she had literally collided with him at the water cooler. She wasn't sure if she imagined it or not, but he had appeared shaken at her nearness, and for a brief second she thought he was going to reach out and take her into his arms. Instead, he had nodded curtly and strode off down the long corridor. Her heart had fluttered wildly all day long.

Sam finished her sandwich and tossed the waxed paper and half a deli pickle into the trash can when Charlie Conway's voice shouted for her attention. "Orion, do me a favor, will you? I can't seem to locate that confounded office boy. Take Mr. Delaney's lunch in to him and set it up."

"Charlie, isn't there someone else...? What I mean is, I can't do...go...in there...Lizzie—can't Lizzie do it?" She felt like a rabbit caught suddenly in a snare. She wanted desperately to see the handsome publisher, wanted desperately to... "I can't do it, Charlie!" Sam bleated.

"Guts, Orion. You can do it. You *will* do it. That's an order. Now, move it!"

Sam picked up the plastic tray with Christian Delaney's lunch on it and carried it precariously down the long corridor that led to his office. The door was partially open and she debated a second before kicking lightly with the toe of her shoe to announce her arrival.

Christian Delaney's back was to Sam as she placed the tray on the neat, uncluttered desk. She was just removing the napkin from the sandwich tray when he swiveled abruptly and knocked her off balance. The ham and rye and the two halves of the kosher pickle slid across the desk. In her attempt to reach for them, she leaned too close and fell into Christian's lap. This couldn't be happening to her. It was. Strong arms held her close, too close.

"This is one way of announcing your arrival. A simple 'Here's your lunch' would have worked just as well." The voice was controlled, with no hint of amusement in it.

Sam felt herself drain of all color. Why did she feel so weak, so...trapped? The viselike hold on her arms hadn't lessened. Her senses reeled with the scent of the man holding her. This was what she wanted, what she needed—to be near him, to have him hold her and whisper sweet words. Evidently, he was expecting her to make some comment or he would have released her. "You moved...I wasn't expecting...Charlie said there...I'm sorry," Sam muttered. In her agitation in trying to defend herself, she found herself cheek to cheek with the man holding her.

Silvery-gray eyes stared into hers, drawing her into their depths. Sam waited, wild anticipation coursing through her like a riptide. She knew he was going to kiss her, and she made no move to extricate herself from his strong hold. His lips were feather light upon her own and she responded in kind. It was Christian who withdrew first, his eyes blazing into her own. Before she could draw a breath, his lips seared hers, sending fire through her veins. When he released her a second time, she was shaken to her very being. He must care for her; otherwise, how could he kiss her like this? Her heart soared and then plummeted when she heard his next words as he somehow thrust her from him, still keeping his hold on her arm. His voice was cold and clipped. "That was a mistake, and I apologize. Have the office boy get me another sandwich." She was dismissed.

Sam shook her head slightly to clear it. Her eyes narrowed. He had done it to her again. He had humiliated her and, worse yet, he had taken advantage of her by kissing her. Never mind that she had wanted him to kiss her, even willed it. An angry retort rose to her lips. His cold eyes were mocking her as she turned on her heel. "Yes sir, Mr. Delaney, sir." At the door she clicked her heels and snapped a salute.

The publisher's deep, mocking laugh followed her all the way back to her office. It wasn't till an hour later that she remembered to order him another sandwich. Christian Delaney wouldn't starve—he ate people alive, especially photo-journalists.

Her desk cleared for the day, Sam spent the remaining minutes watching the hands on the wall clock creep toward the five and twelve. Soon it would be time to go home and spend another lonely evening watching television. She knew she could work on the painting of Christian, but all the life seemed to have gone out of the project. The plain and simple truth of the matter was she couldn't bear to even pick up a brush.

Christian Delaney's voice thundered over the partition. "There must be someone around here. Where's the assignment sheet? Lizzie," he roared, "where's Matowskie? Where's Blandenberg? And what happened to Jefferies and Arbeiter? Well?"

Sam rose and stood in the doorway. If the angry publisher thought he was cowing Lizzie, he was mistaken. His arrogant, insufferable attitude only worked on dimwits like herself. The man hadn't been born who could cow Lizzie.

"Matowskie is in Seattle. You sent him yourself three days ago. Blandenberg is in Israel on vacation. You approved it yourself three weeks ago. Jefferies and Arbeiter are covering an assignment in Venezuela. If you're looking for a photographer, there's one standing right behind you." Lizzie's tone was saccharine sweet, yet firm. She ran the company, and no upstart like Christian Delaney was going to intimidate her. Besides, she was sixty-nine years old, and rank did have its privileges.

Sam's heart started to pound and then she started to bristle. Just let him ignore her this time. Now she was angry. Whatever the assignment was, she wanted it. How could he turn her down this time? He couldn't. If she was all there was, he had to use her. It never occurred to her to even wonder what and where the assignment was.

The publisher's eyes went from Lizzie to Charlie Conway to Sam. He didn't bother with more than a cursory glance in her direction before he locked in with Charlie Conway. "Order the Lear jet to be made ready. The board decided that with the feedback coming in so steadily from the Mideast, we're going to take a crack at the energy problem from here. The destination is the Southwest. You're it, Orion."

Lizzie answered for her. "That's what she's here for. Two hours, Orion. Be at the airport."

"Who...who's going with me?" Sam stammered. Not that she cared. She didn't care about anything except that Christian

Delaney had said she could go, that he was giving her the assignment, and Lizzie, God bless her, approved. If Christian assigned her to cover Dracula's castle, she couldn't have cared less.

"Me," came the curt reply.

Sam swallowed hard and then she grinned from ear to ear. "You got it, Mr. Delaney." Now let him make whatever he wanted out of that statement. She was going to the Southwest with him. Together, in one plane. They would be working side by side. Truth was truth. She was going to have him all to herself, and by some stroke of luck she just might be able to convince him of a few things. Whatever, she had a fighting chance now, and she was going to make the most of it.

Lizzie favored Sam with a heavy-lidded wink, and Charlie Conway shifted his evil-smelling stogie to the left side of his mouth.

Chapter Five

Sam hadn't really known what to expect when she arrived at the private airstrip on the outskirts of Baltimore, where she was to meet Christian Delaney to embark on their assignment of American energy resources, but the shining Lear jet, with its engines whining in warm-up, certainly wasn't it. And when she lugged her camera equipment and duffel bag out to the winged machine and curiously looked into the cockpit for a glimpse of the pilot, Christian answered her unspoken question.

"I'm a qualified pilot, Orion. This little beauty is all mine. Personal property; not an asset of Delaney Enterprises."

Samantha felt herself flush with anger. She wanted this assignment, but at what price? Was he going to be caustic and riddle her with his sarcasm during the entire trip? Holding back a tart reply, she threw her duffel up the gangplank and into the plane. Forcing a smile to her lips, she turned to meet his stare. "She is a beauty, Mr. Delaney, and I have every confidence in your ability as a pilot."

"Good. Then you won't mind sitting up front with me." His eyes watched her, daring her to demur.

Sam's spirits sank lower. She wanted nothing more at this point than to hide away somewhere near the tail of the plane, far away from this man who created such conflicting emotions in her. This job would necessitate working very closely with him to complete the assignment. Was she prepared to be so near him, close enough to touch, and yet, at the same time, recoiling from his presence? Inhaling deeply, as though breathing in the courage she would need, Sam reminded herself that this very same man who held such a great attraction for her was the one and the same who refused to believe her innocence concerning Gemini's will.

"I'd enjoy sitting up front," she heard herself say lightly, refusing to meet his eyes, fearful that the lie would show itself there in the windows of her soul.

"Good. Got everything? We won't be anywhere near a drugstore where you can buy flash bulbs or anything else."

Samantha bristled in spite of her resolve not to allow him to get to her. "Mr. Delaney, I'm a professional. I assure you I've got everything I need."

Her sharp tone seemed to go unnoticed. "Great. Climb aboard."

The silvery wings reflected the gold of the sun as they leveled off at twenty thousand feet. Christian's command of the Lear was impressive, just as Sam knew it would be. Everything Christian did was with an inborn confidence and certain ability. His hands on the instruments and controls were steady and knowledgeable, and his voice was crisp and authoritative when he called in to the control tower far below.

Their first destination was a uranium mining plant in southwestern Arizona. Hours alone with Christian Delaney.

"There's a coffee maker in the back. Want to try your hand at it?"

Wordlessly, Sam unhitched herself from the seatbelt and, stooping slightly, made her way into the body of the plane and to a small counter near the tail section. Everything she needed was readily available, including coffee cream in the small refrigerator beneath the shiny counter.

As she waited for the coffee to brew, Sam sat and chewed at her thumbnail, realizing a sense of tension drain out of her. Just being near Christian set her teeth on edge. There was a sorrow that settled somewhere between her second and third rib because he believed she was a fortune hunter of the worst kind. There was nothing to say and nothing she could do to convince him that she hadn't preyed upon an old woman's sentiments.

The coffee maker gurgled and indicated its cycle was completed. She prepared two mugs, remembering Christian preferred cream, no sugar. Cautiously, she made her way forward again and handed him the steaming mug. For an instant their fingers touched, and Sam felt a bolt of electricity shoot through her. How long had it been since he had touched her? How long since he had taken her in his arms and claimed her mouth for his own? Ages. Centuries past a lifetime.

Slowly, she sipped her coffee, covertly watching Christian's every movement. She realized his casual expertise in handling the plane. How confident he was. How masterful. It was little wonder that he had come to loathe her. This was an open, straightforward man who was used to taking up the reins of responsibility. Lies and deceit had no place in his life. He would never believe that she had tried to tell him the truth about her identity time and time again. And now, she had begun to wonder just how hard she had tried. Was it possible that she had unconsciously allowed him to interrupt her every time she was about to tell him that she was Sam Blakely? Had she been so greedy for his kisses that it had jeopardized her own honesty?

For what was beginning to seem like a lifetime, Samantha sat beside Christian Delaney while their plane headed due West, and the plains of America rolled beneath them. The publisher's silence was deafening. He hated her, she was certain of it. There was no use trying to explain her relationship with his Aunt Gemini and the fact that she hadn't even realized the old woman's connection with Delaney Enterprises, much less connived to dupe her into writing her into the will.

If Samantha had somehow hoped that this time alone with Christian would be an opportunity to mend the wounds, she knew now how wrong she had been. She knew if Christian would turn to look at her his eyes would be shards of steel and his face would be a mask of granite.

She surveyed his uncompromising concentration out the windshield and toward the horizon. Could this be the same man who had swept her off her feet—the same man who possessed her lips with his own? Who had promised her tender moments with his eyes and offered her shelter and a loving haven with his arms?

Why didn't he say something? Anything! How could he expect to complete an assignment under these circumstances? Silently, she willed him to turn and speak to her. Instead, he fixed his steely gray eyes straight ahead and his mouth into a thin, forbidding line. He held her in contempt, and now that same contempt was filling the cockpit and choking off her air.

Sam massaged her temples, warding off a migraine. She watched Christian's every movement and saw his casual expertise in handling the plane. Samantha found it impossible to tear her eyes away from him. She memorized his profile, the arrogant set of his head above broad shoulders and powerful body. She knew every nuance of his features. Knew them and loved them. She had loved this man long before she ever knew him. Long, patient hours of working on his portrait into the lonely hours of the night when only she and his likeness shared the solitude.

She loved him. Didn't he know that? Couldn't he sense it? Feel it? How could he be so stupid and insensitive? Did he think only of the fact that Gemini Delaney had made a ridiculous gesture by willing her that large interest in the family business?

Guilty tears stung her eyes. She had had opportunities to confess to him that she was the Sam Blakely he was seeking. But she had let them go by. And now, when she had finally told him, it was too late. She had made him feel like a fool for not having known much sooner. Little wonder he thought she was a fortune hunter.

A sudden jolt shook Samantha out of her reverie. Her eyes flew to the left wing, where the engine was issuing a cloud of black smoke. Her stomach lurched warningly. She sought Christian with her eyes; panic welled within her. She saw the tenseness in his shoulders and neck and the hard set of his mouth.

"Christian! What's wrong?"

"How do I know?" he growled from between clenched teeth. "But if we're going to crash, it's not going to be from twenty thousand feet up. Hold on, I'm taking her down."

Samantha felt the pressure in her ears as the craft descended and the ground below came closer and closer. "Where are we?" she gulped, looking for the gray skyline of a city.

"We've been out over the desert for the past hour. That's California straight ahead, Arizona below.

"Better hold on tight, Orion. Take the flotation cushion from under your seat and put it in your lap. Get your head down, way down!" His tone compelled her into immediate action.

She heard Christian try to make radio contact and send a May Day signal. It was all happening so fast, as fast as the rush of air against the windshield as the Lear plummeted toward the earth. She heard Christian swear, trying again and again to make contact, muttering something about an elec-

trical burnout in the instrument panel.
"Hold on, Orion, we're going down!"

Long moments. Eternity. Pressure in the
cockpit dropped. Her ears popped. A lifetime of prayers skated through her mind,
and every one of them included Christian.

She felt the aircraft's speed decrease until
she thought they must be hovering in midair. Suddenly, she felt as though the floor-
boards beneath her feet were rattling,
shaking, grinding against something. The
wheels touched the ground and the plane
seemed to skid through the whirling dust as
it swooshed and careened wildly. Samantha's heart was in her mouth as she pressed
her head down and felt the safety belt dig
into her abdomen, holding her back against
the seat when the momentum was hurling
her forward.

A terrible wrenching sound filled her
world as the Lear tilted crazily to one side.
She heard Christian swear again under his
breath and the thunderous noise in her ears
subsided as he cut the engines.

Cautiously, incredulously, Samantha
raised her head from the cushion. They were

on the ground, and although they were tilted to one side, all forward motion had ceased. They were safe!

"This is your captain speaking." Christian laughed with wild relief from where he slumped back against his seat. "At this time I'd like to thank you for flying blind, and *Daylight Magazine* thanks you and hopes your stay in the Arizona desert will be enjoyable. I'd like to say, at this time, that the temperature is a pleasant one hundred ten degrees. Be certain to gather all your belongings and check the overhead racks so nothing is left behind."

Sam unsnapped the seatbelt and crawled across the cockpit, throwing her arms around Christian. "I knew you could do it! I knew it! I prayed for both of us!" she cried, planting a wet kiss on his cheek, his nose, his eyes, and finally his mouth.

Hard hands closed around her arms, pushing her away. "Am I really to believe you prayed for the both of us, or just yourself, Orion? Think how much simpler it would be to take over Delaney Enterprises if I wasn't around to stop you!"

This couldn't be happening to her. She must be having a nightmare. When she awakened, all would be well. No, it wouldn't. Nothing was ever going to be right again. An invisible ramrod stiffened in her spine and she locked glares with her accuser. "No matter what I say or how I explain, you aren't going to believe me. I don't have to defend myself, Christian—not to you or to anyone else. You've already judged and found me guilty. I'm sorry for both of us that whatever it was we had wasn't strong enough to weather this." Was that cool, positive voice really hers? Now, when the end of her world was looming before her? The ramrod in her spine slipped beneath Christian's silvery, unblinking stare.

"Get your gear together, Orion. We can't stay here. As the captain of this plane, consider that an order. This is not time for hysterics." His voice was controlled, but there was a thinly veiled note of venom beneath it. Clearly, she had no choice but to follow his orders.

Christian hefted himself from his awkward position in the crazily lopsided cockpit and literally had to crawl through the hatch to the rear of the plane. Silently, he emptied the small refrigerator of soft drinks and a small supply of canned goods. He searched the compartment over the seats and found the one containing the first-aid kit and flashlight.

Red-faced, Sam watched him, knowing that she herself would have set out into the desert without a thought to the supplies to be found aboard the aircraft. Even in crisis, Christian kept his head. And now, here alone in the wilderness, it suddenly dawned upon her that she was completely dependent upon him. Somehow, the thought was not comforting.

The heat was oppressive. By shading her eyes, Sam could see Christian striding ahead in the distance. Her heart thudded and then was still. If she wanted to catch up and not lose sight of him, she was going to have to pick up her pace. And, she told herself, he had the food and drinks, not to mention the compass she had seen him discover in the first-aid kit.

Quickening her steps over the hard-packed sand, Sam seemed to be gaining on Christian's retreating figure. Keeping up that long-legged stride might have tired him. Or else he was deliberately slowing down so she could catch up with him. She only wanted to keep him in sight; she didn't want to walk beside him.

Sam's pace slackened as she wiped the perspiration from her brow and dabbed at her neck with the tail of her shirt. This heat was worse than anything she had ever experienced. Her mouth was full of cotton balls and gritty sand. The minuscule grains were in her eyebrows and her hair, and her skin itched. She wished for a drink but would die before asking him for one of the sodas he had taken from the plane.

Suddenly, Sam's heart thumped madly as she saw Christian turn to glance at her over his shoulder. He stopped and faced her, concern written on his features. Coming abreast of him, Sam shaded her eyes against the golden glare of the sun.

"Give me your duffel, Orion." Obediently, she handed him the soft-sided bag.

Dropping to one knee, she watched him rifle through it, withdrawing a spare shirt. "Here, wrap this around your head to protect you from the sun."

Clumsily, Sam struggled with the shirt, finding it impossible to do as he ordered. "You've already had too much sun," he said solemnly, taking the garment from her and doing it for her.

"I'd like to offer you something to drink, but we have to conserve whatever we have. Here, take this." He stooped to pick up a smooth pebble from near her feet, wiped it off on his shirt, and offered it to her. "Put this in your mouth. It's an old Indian trick to fool the salivary glands and bring moisture to the mouth." Sam did as ordered and, while it didn't produce the hoped-for results, her mouth didn't feel so parched.

"We'll stop now and rest. We'll continue for a few hours when the sun begins to set. Since I'm responsible for you, you'll do as I instruct. Understood?"

Samantha nodded in agreement, grateful for the opportunity to get off her burning feet. The heat was coming off the sand and penetrating her hiking boots, and she wished for a cool pool of water to put them in.

Christian led her over to a bone-dry, scrubby-looking bush of indistinct genus and faced her away from the sun. He placed the duffel under her head and ordered her to stay put. Then, taking himself to the opposite side of the bush, he settled himself down.

Tired though she was, she hesitated lying back and succumbing to sleep. She wasn't certain that Christian wouldn't leave without her, and she admitted to herself that she was afraid he might. What would she do if he took it into his head that she was more trouble than she was worth, and he left her here alone? She couldn't sleep—she didn't dare.

Back home, when she couldn't sleep, she would get out of bed and work in her darkroom or go through the stacks of old pictures she had collected. Or work on Christian's portrait, she reminded herself bleakly. Quietly, she withdrew the prized camera and squinted into the sun. Why not? There was nothing else to do, and she had a

generous supply of film in her gadget bag.
Why not take pictures of the desert? When
she looked at them in years to come, she
would remember. It wasn't fair. How could
this be happening to her? There he was,
mighty male animal, sleeping like a baby,
and she had to stay awake because she was
afraid he would leave her.

Sam focused the lens and adjusted her
f-stop. She moved slowly, striving for the
correct light. She turned, her intention being to snap a picture of the sleeping publisher. His features were relaxed in sleep,
making him look vulnerable. Only she knew
what kind of lurking monster was hidden
behind those handsome features. Quickly,
she snapped again and again. In those years
to come she could quietly torture herself by
staring at his likeness. Tears burned her eyes
unexpectedly. Her feelings were too raw, too
injured, to make logical thought possible.

Feeling her eyes upon him, Christian woke
up with a start. He glared at her and kept his
silence. Samantha felt compelled to explain.
"You looked so vulnerable, so peaceful . . . I
only wanted to capture it on film."

"A likely excuse. What you probably meant to do was bash me over the head and then you'd meet little resistance to holding on to that fifty-one percent," Christian snarled. "Well, I have news for you, Miss Photographer, you won't get rid of me that easily."

"Is that what you think? Of all the stupid, insufferable...you're detestable! I can't even look at you!" she shot back.

"You have that a little backward. It's you who's detestable. Imagine, taking advantage of a little old lady. It's criminal, do you know that? Criminal!"

"Think whatever you like. As long as I know I didn't do anything, I can live with myself and that fifty-one percent!" she cried savagely. "The only thing I was guilty of is...was...not explaining the mixup in the first place. Change that to the only *stupid* thing I was guilty of. I grant you the whole situation appears decidedly suspicious, but you won't give me a chance to explain."

"Explain! No thank you," Christian said sourly. "I've had enough lies to last me a lifetime. Besides, I know my Aunt Gemini was nobody's fool, yet you seemed to have managed to talk her out of the controlling interest in the family business. Heaven only knows what you'd try to talk me out of before this trek through the desert is over."

Sam backed off a step, hardly believing what she had heard. She flinched as though she had been physically struck. She wouldn't cry; she refused to give him that satisfaction. Besides, when you were dead inside, everything stopped working, even tears.

Christian Delaney wasn't finished upbraiding her. "And when we get back to Washington, consider yourself dismissed. Don't even bother coming into the office. You're through!"

The words and his anger vibrated along Sam's nerve endings and she felt her fingers curl into claws. The invisible ramrod in her spine stiffened. "You can't fire me! I didn't do anything! I'm good at what I do, and you know it!"

He leaped to his feet and stared down at her, his mouth fixed into an implacable line of fury. "I don't know any such thing. It's my magazine, and I don't want you to have any part of it.'' His voice had dropped two octaves and held a barely controlled rage. He was an imposing figure, glaring down at her: tall, lean, powerful.

"I have an unbreakable contract. Gemini saw to that. You try to fire me and I go to court. I'll charge you with sexual harassment!'' What was she saying? Was she crazy? At the malevolent expression on his face, Sam stepped backward.

Christian blanched. His fury was barely controlled. His white knuckled fist reached down and picked up his canvas bag and slung it over his shoulder. Turning away from her, he stomped off, dark head lowered over hunched shoulders.

Following behind at a safe distance, Sam seethed inwardly. Had she really said all those things? From the expression on his face, she had not only said them, but he had believed her. As if she would ever do any such thing. She didn't want his company or his money. She had lashed out in self-defense, aiming to stun him, hurt him. Any mean and hateful thought that had flown into her head, she had spit out through her mouth. It was one thing to defend herself, to hurt someone, but it had been totally unnecessary to keep sticking in the knife and twisting it for emphasis.

"There's one other thing, Mr. Delaney," she called to his retreating back. "I want to go on record as saying that I detest people who have the power to shatter other people's dreams and then actually go ahead and do it. You are one of those people! First, you let Gemini down by putting your business first instead of being there at the end when she needed you. And now you suspect the worst about me and refuse to listen to any explanation."

Even as she watched him, he stopped dead in his tracks. Every muscle in his body tensed and he was ready to spring like a wild jungle cat. Fear balled up in her throat, choking off all air. She had gone too far. Reminding him that he hadn't been home in time for Gemini's last days and then her funeral had been a low blow, and it didn't appear he was going to take it lying down.

Paralyzed with terror, she saw him turn. He placed one foot in front of the other, stalking her. Unable to move, unable to think, she was mesmerized by his approach. Threatening, lethal, determined, he closed the distance between them. Powerful, potent and ruthless, he sighted his quarry and hypnotized her with the predatory glare in his silver-gray eyes as though she were a jackrabbit paralyzed by oncoming headlights.

Samantha gasped for breath and felt the shock of motion return to her limbs. She turned and ran, throwing one leg in front of the other, escaping, scrambling away as though a hound of hell were on her heels. And he was.

Her feet slipped in the sand; her breath came in ragged gasps. Her duffel and camera bag banged against her legs in an unrelenting rhythm. Just when she thought that her heart would burst, she felt herself being pulled backward and her legs sprawling out at awkward angles.

Together they rolled over the shifting sands. He bore his weight on top of her, stilling her struggles. She was locked against his heaving chest, feeling his labored breaths against the side of her face.

She felt him draw away, felt his gaze upon her. Panic tearing through her, she cautioned a glance at his face. His eyes were burning through her to her very core. Fear subsided; there was no menace in his silver-shadowed glance now. Instead, there was something else there, something she didn't dare put a name to.

With a force that was almost violent in its intent, he covered her body with his own. Pressing down, bearing down, stilling her struggles and kicks, he held her, dragging her arms upward over her head to prevent her from tearing at his face. Her breathing came in pants and ended in an inconsolable groan of hopelessness.

Deliberately, with barely concealed menace, Christian glared down at his prey. He studied her face for a long, unendurably long moment. Their eyes locked—hers with trepidation, and his with victory. He lowered his head, aware that she was incapable of movement, and his mouth came crashing down upon hers.

The desert sand shifted beneath her weight, and Christian shifted his length to hold her captive. His lips possessed hers and awakened her already heightened senses. Samantha's world became full of Christian. The taste of him, the feel of him, the power of him—they all assaulted her awareness. His sensual demands excited and aroused and ignited her passions.

The heat of the sun was dimmed by the desire that blazed between them. His intimate exploration of her mouth sent tingles of pleasure down her spine. His hands released her arms, allowing them to wind around his neck, holding embracing, answering his.

The touch of his hands aroused and inspired a slow curl of heat that emanated from her offered body and consumed them. He tasted her flesh, where her shirt revealed it, all the way down to the soft swell of her heaving breasts.

His excursion of the smooth curves of her body was sure and designed to please, as though they had roamed and discovered many times before this. The fires licked at

Samantha's senses, tearing down her defenses, allowing her to forget all else besides being here, this minute, with Christian, loving Christian.

She had never felt so alive, so vibrant, as she did when she was in his arms, and she knew with a certainty that the only death that would ever exist for her was to be separated from this man who could sizzle her passions and awaken her desires.

His fingers were in her hair, on her throat, teasing the pleasure points beneath her ear. Each of his movements was created and drafted to overwhelm her and to ensure his complete and total possession. A tide of desire ebbed over her objections. There were no objections. There was nothing—only Christian, the man she loved and wanted.

Her back arched, her arms held him close, her lips answered his, and when she felt him draw back and roll over, pulling her with him, she gladly followed. Their legs tangled, their breath mingled, and with a wanton abandonment she undid the buttons of her shirt, allowing him complete access to the heated flesh beneath. With authority his fingers wound through the silky strands of her hair, pulling her head back while his lips made a heady progression along her throat to the valley between her breasts.

Desire became a fire, white-hot and searing them together in a wild and lusty experimentation of lips and hands. On top of him as she was, she was aware of his lean, muscular body between her knees. She felt the sun burn into the newly exposed skin of her back, matched only by the even hotter touch of Christian's lips on her breasts.

Samantha looked down into his eyes, feeling as though she was bathed in molten silver and golden sands. A hidden spring of emotion bubbled to the surface as she whispered, ''I never knew love could be like this.''

Suddenly, she felt him stiffen beneath her. His hands ceased their tender excursion of her flesh, and his mouth, pressed against hers, became hard and unyielding. Pulling away, staring down into his face, she saw his gray eyes harden and become like forged steel.

"Love, Orion? I thought you called it sexual harassment!"

Sam pulled away from him and struggled to her knees. Wounded beyond belief, she fumbled with the buttons of her shirt, covering herself from his scrutiny. How could she have been so stupid? Did she want this man so much that she could forget her own self-respect?

Christian narrowed his eyes to slits. She watched his lips tighten into a grim, white line. "Why were you taking pictures of me?" he demanded.

A sob rose to Sam's throat. If she answered him, he would know how close to tears she was. She turned her face to the side and clenched her hands into tiny fists.

"I asked you a question. Answer me!" Christian thundered.

Through superhuman effort she submerged a sob. If she could only stop her body from trembling. Her mind raced; she would not, not ever, admit to this man that she had wanted his picture so she could remember him when he was most vulnerable.

Christian lunged suddenly, reaching out a long arm and pulling her against his massive chest. Samantha's face was within a hair's breadth of his. Fascinated, she watched a muscle twitch in his cheek. He was holding her much too tight—too tight to breathe. Her breath was coming in short, ragged gasps as Christian cupped her head, with its tousled hair, in his big hand, forcing it back at an awkward angle. His voice was soft and full of menace as he stared down into her tear-moistened eyes.

"You would have allowed me to make love to you a moment ago," he said huskily. He thrust her from him; his voice was tight and bitter. "It won't work, Orion. If you don't believe or accept anything else, believe that I will never permit you to take control of Delaney Enterprises."

Anger and humiliation ripped through Samantha. She didn't deserve this treatment, but she had no defense. He would never believe her, no matter what she said or what she did. She wanted to lash out at him, tell him that she would have given herself to him because she loved him. Not money or his publishing empire. Only Christian. The words never found their way to her lips. She could only stand there with her eyes cast down at the dry, arid ground, and only sheer determination helped her choke back the tears.

A long moment of silence crept between them as he waited for her answer. His eyes bore through her expectantly, and when Samantha found the courage to meet them, she was surprised to find a dark yearning in his gaze. But it was fleeting, and when he decided she had no reasonable answer for her actions, he turned away.

Tears were flowing wildly down Sam's cheeks as she stuffed the camera into its case. She was careful to keep her back to Christian so he wouldn't see how vulnerable she really was. She couldn't allow him to find her with her defenses down again. The hurt was too great, too crippling.

Sam's tears and stuffy nose were replaced with hiccups as she trudged behind Christian. The only thing that made the trek bearable was the pleasure she was going to have when she handed over the sealed envelope in the publisher's own safe. She'd tear the check up before his very eyes. Then she would tear up her contract with *Daylight Magazine*. If Christian Delaney didn't want her, then she didn't want him, either! Even as she thought it, a fresh wave of hiccups seized her, punishing her for the lie. She would spend her life wanting Christian Delaney, and she knew it.

Chapter Six

Samantha was surprised how chill and cold the nights in the desert could become after the broiling heat of the day. She and Christian were camped for the night beside a rare outcropping of ancient rocks that still managed, somehow, to hold a little of the sun's heat. They both knew it was a temporary state of affairs since the sun had only gone down a little over an hour ago, and soon those same rocks would be clammy and cold—as cold as the stars that were beginning to twinkle in the velvet blackness of the night.

Her scanty knowledge of outdoor living seemed grossly inadequate now, when it was really being put to the test. Thank goodness for Christian. He, at least, had had the foresight to realize they would need a fire for warmth, if not for the light. So, during their interminable walk he had instructed her to gather dried vegetation when it was available. Their northeast journey had taken them closer to the foothills where the terrain had given way from loose sand to a rocky foundation. There was much more protection from winds and an ample supply of dried, scrubby bushes whose underbrush snapped off easily in the hand.

Working together, they gathered rocks to make a fire ring, and with the cigarette lighter from his pocket, they ignited the brush, feeding the fire from time to time to maintain it.

She was silent as she watched Christian work, and she wondered if he felt she was foolish because she didn't think of this small comfort herself. Out of his duffel he withdrew several packages of cheese crackers and an already-opened can of soda. It was tonic water, and the bitter liquid was more refreshing to their thirst than the sweeter soda that Christian had also taken from the plane's small refrigerator.

Sam settled down on the far side of the fire and after a moment Christian brought her the first-aid kit he had retrieved from the compartment over the seats. "Poke through this, will you, Orion? I've already taken the compass out, and that's what we've been following. Maybe there's something else we could use." Sam looked up, surprised by the almost friendly tone of his voice. Maybe, just maybe, if there was nothing else they could salvage of their relationship, they could develop a camaraderie and help each other through this uncertain situation of being stranded in the desert, miles away from anywhere.

Her hopes were dashed when Christian spoke again. "That's woman's stuff; I don't know a bandage from a snake-bite kit."

Angrily, Sam snapped open the metal lid. Of all the chauvinistic... just because she had long hair and wore lipstick didn't signify that all she was good for was "woman's work"!

First of all, there was a second compass. Wordlessly, she tossed it over to Christian, who immediately checked it against the one in his pocket and nodded his head confidently. Next, Sam dug out a first-aid cream for small cuts. Happily, she opened the plastic tube and smeared the soothing lotion on her weather-dried face, satisfied with the immediate results. Since they had suffered no injuries, not even minor scratches, she had no immediate use for the various ointments and iodines and bandages. But at the bottom, folded into a flat rectangle, enclosed in an envelope of clear plastic, was a shock blanket—a thin, aluminum-gray nylon sheet designed to keep in thermal body heat. It would appear the nights wouldn't be so cold, after all. Happily, she displayed her find to Christian. "You take it," he told her. "I'll make do with the extra clothes in my duffel."

The extra shirts and light jacket which were stowed in her duffel bag were further protection against the cold. She may have to go to sleep hungry and tired, but she wouldn't be cold. As Christian banked the fire, Sam wearily made a pillow of her duffel bag and tried to assume a comfortable position to sleep. The shock blanket was light, but within a few minutes she happily admitted that it lived up to its purpose. Turning on her side, she was soon fast asleep.

Sometime during the early morning hours, when the sun was just creeping over the horizon, Samantha awoke with a start. Something was holding her and preventing her from rolling over onto her back. Christian. Apparently, the cold night air had had its effect on him, and he decided to share the shock blanket with her.

His arm was flung carelessly around her in sleep, the tips of his fingers just resting on the swell of her breasts. His body had molded itself around her in sleep, and they were nested together like two spoons. His breath feathered against her cheek, and she realized that somehow, during the night, in their exhausted sleep, he had slipped his arm beneath her head and she was resting on his shoulder. For a long, glorious moment, Samantha knew the joy of awakening in the arms of the man she loved. *Did love,* she corrected. She couldn't, wouldn't allow her defenses to slip now. Knowing what being devastatingly hurt by Christian's unrelenting suspicions could do to her, she was not going to put herself in that position again. To contradict the adage, once was certainly enough!

Christian seemed to sense her wakefulness, or had he already been awake and watching her sleep. The thought was disconcerting and Sam flushed as she thought of how his fingertips had rested so close to her breasts.

"Rise and shine, Orion. We've got a long day ahead of us."

Obediently, she hauled herself out from under the shock blanket and away from his embrace. Immediately, the morning air felt chill and hostile. Or was it just because she had moved away from this man whose masterful confidence in even the most precarious of situations could make her feel protected and secure?

They decided to save a few remaining packages of crackers and cheese for later and broke camp to travel while the air was still cool. Mile after mile, Sam trudged along behind Christian. His tall, straight back became a directional for her, a beacon in the vastness of the desert. She found she was capable of losing all track of time. Glancing at her watch time and again, she realized how slowly the minutes passed when one was miserable and exhausted. She rolled the smooth pebble around in her mouth—having decided it did help—and thought about the two remaining cans of warm soda in his duffel.

The sun had reached its apex, and Christian was searching for a spot of shade where they could rest through the worst heat of the day. He was less than successful, finding only a low stand of sun-burned, leafless trees that had probably been around since the time of Christ.

"This will have to do. Take something out of that duffel and cover your head." He had already stripped off his shirt and draped it, Arab fashion, over his own head.

Following instructions, Samantha then dropped to the ground and lay down with her arm over her eyes. The thought of the wonderfully wet soda was becoming an obsession. After a few minutes she sat up, knowing her sudden movement was noticed by Christian. Working fast and furiously, she dug through her duffel and withdrew the shock blanket and the first-aid kit.

Reading her thoughts, Christian jumped to his feet, and together they carefully laid the blanket over the stunted trees, securing it at the corners with gauze bandage. Sam noted how well they worked together in an amiable silence. Once or twice their hands touched, and Samantha felt as though she'd been jolted by an electric charge. Whatever she felt for this man, it definitely was not indifference.

Settled close together in the shade they had created, they shared a few sips of the precious soda. It didn't quench their thirst, but it was wet.

They continued their march through the coolest part of the day, when the reds and golds of the sun slanted across the ground, making long, dark shadows of every bush and rock. When the sun dipped below the horizon, and it became too dark to walk safely, they again set up camp. This time, Christian gathered the rocks to make a fire circle while Sam scrounged for dry wood.

When Sam was digging through the duffel, the unmistakable sound of metal against metal clinked.

That night they felt as though they'd feasted like kings: half a can of soda, a package of crackers, and half a can of deviled ham. The icy stars twinkled down on them, seeming friendlier than the night before.

Once again, Christian banked the fire so it would burn slowly throughout the night. Sam settled herself down, and placing her head on the duffel, she lay back and threw the thin shock blanket over her.

A moment later Christian crawled in beside her and, back to back, they drifted off to sleep.

Sometime during the night Sam awakened to find her head nestled on Christian's broad shoulder and her arm thrown care-

lessly over his chest. Her right leg was cra-
dled between both of his, and he held her
lightly in an embrace. It was dark, too dark
to see him. The fire had almost completely
gone out, and the desert night air on her face
was cool in contrast to the warmth they gen-
erated beneath the blanket. But she knew
somehow that Christian was not asleep. She
sensed his awareness as though it were a
tangible thing.

"You sleeping?" she heard him whisper.
She remained silent, pretending sleep. If she
admitted she was awake, she would have to
move, have to take her arm from around him
and take her head from his chest. She listened, hearing the thump of his heart, hearing the slow intake of his breath.

It was peaceful, so peaceful, and they
cuddled together beneath the blanket as
though they'd slept together for every night
of their lives.

Tenderly, he turned to face her; she could
feel his breath upon her cheek. Softly, softer
than the night air, he grazed her cheek with
his lips.

More than anything, she wanted to turn, capture his lips with her own, taste his kiss and feel his arms tighten around her. But the thought of him accusing her of seducing him, of trapping him, of making love to him and making him love her just to get her hands on his money and the Delaney empire was too great. Her humiliation would be beyond bearing.

Still feigning sleep, Samantha sighed deeply and turned over on her side, facing away from Christian. In the darkness, she squeezed her eyes shut and a single tear of regret escaped from behind her long, upswept lashes.

Christian stirred, turning toward her, snuggling close, his body pressed against hers, spoon fashion. His arm wrapped around her and she relished the comforting warmth, the gentle gesture. Long into the night, to the first break of dawn, Samantha lay quietly, determined to remember this gentle truce into the long, dark future.

Four more days passed and the quiet truce between Samantha and Christian continued. But just beneath the surface, lying like a tiger stalking its prey, were the differences between them. Samantha had surrendered the need to explain about Gemini, and Christian didn't mention it.

The Hasselblad camera she had inherited from her father became part of a game they played. During the day whenever an interesting ground formation or light study came to Samantha's attention, she stopped, took out the camera, and snapped away. She took several pictures of Christian as their journey progressed and he had come to the point where he even good-naturedly posed for her. He had sprouted a scrubby beard, and his hair was unkempt, as were his clothes. But he now sported a wonderful bronze tan that resembled newly minted copper.

Samantha herself had traded her long-sleeved khaki shirt and slacks for a brief costume of halter top and shorts for an hour or so each morning, and Christian's tan was rivaled only by her own.

The first-aid cream she had found in the kit was a wonderful protection against the drying hcat of the sun as far as her face was concerned. She was determined not to return to Washington dried out like a prune, with only her hands and face kissed by the sun. She supposed she was being foolish, and Christian called her a sun worshipper, but vanity won out.

Several times when they stopped at noonday, she had entrusted her camera to Christian and he snapped pictures of her while she posed for him. They laughed that when they finally returned to D.C. and looked at the pictures, it would seem as though they had shared a vacation in the sun. Samantha fleetingly wondered if his casual statement meant that the wounds between them were healing.

Chapter Seven

Early morning stars were still visible in the sky when Christian awakened her. Dragging herself from sleep, Samantha was forced to leave the warmth of the thin blanket. While Christian went about covering the fire with loose earth, she quickly ran a brush through her hair and straightened her clothing.

"If I'm correct," Christian said, breaking the silence, "we should be out of this wilderness within the next two days. California should be right over those hills in the distance."

His words should have been encouraging; instead, they filled Sam with a sense of dread. Civilization and home didn't hold the promise she had wished for at the beginning of this adventure when the plane had gone down. Civilization and home now meant being away from Christian. Their camaraderie had developed out of a mutual dependence on one another. Once back home, that relationship would end and Christian would send her out of his life forever.

As they packed their belongings into the two duffels, Christian shook a soft-drink can experimentally, a frown creasing his face. It had taken all their willpower to refrain from emptying the can of its last few sips of liquid. The scowl on his face communicated to Samantha the seriousness of their situation. The distant hills seemed so far away, too far and too long to be without water or some other liquid to ward off total dehydration.

Glancing in her direction and realizing that he had transmitted his worst fears, Christian soothed, "Come on, now, it's not as bad as all that. We're well into the foothills now. There's bound to be a water source, no matter how small.''

Samantha smiled weakly, running her tongue over cracked, dry lips. How would they ever find water in this huge, vast wilderness? The out-croppings of rock were so numerous that they could climb right past a tiny spring and never notice it. It seemed Christian wasn't going to allow her time to worry. He helped her load her duffel, slung her precious camera case over his own shoulder, and pointed her off along the trail they had been following for the past two days.

Hours passed; the sun climbed the sky in a wide, pepper-dry arc. With each hour the trek became more unbearably hot. Even the wind that stirred the dust and threw it in their faces was dry and hot. Still Christian encouraged her to go on. She knew without a doubt that without his strength she could have given up hope days ago, out beneath the burning sun, brain scorched, helpless.

When they stopped to rest later in the afternoon and when they had consumed the last of the too-sweet, flat, nevertheless wet,

soda remaining in the last can, Christian
pulled his navigating map out of his duffel.
As he studied it for the umpteenth time, Samantha saw him look upward, searching the
sky. She knew he couldn't be looking for a
search plane. That possibility had already
been discussed and discarded. The itinerary
had been indefinite, and waiting for someone at *Daylight Magazine* to become concerned about their whereabouts and begin a
search would be foolish. And deadly.

"What are you looking for, Christian?"
she asked as his eyes once again scanned the
bright blue sky.

"Birds."

"Birds? You...you don't mean vul-
tures...do you?" she finished weakly.

"No, birds. They need water, too, you
know, and some of the bigger ones feed on
rabbits and woodchucks, which also need
water. Usually, birds roost near a water supply, and in late afternoon they usually head
home." Even as he spoke, a clutch of high-
flying figures dotted the sky.

"I've been watching them for some time.
According to my map, the treeline of these

foothills is just a little way off. Get it, Orion?
Trees. Birds?''

"Let's go, then," Sam said as she struggled to her feet. "We still have a couple of
hours of daylight to search."

"Atta girl," Christian praised as he helped
her sling her duffel over her shoulder. "Say
a prayer and keep your eye on those birds."

The trek had become more difficult now
that their trail took them on an incline. Soon
Sam was able to see a line of scrubby trees
and the underbrush looked thicker, more
plush, somehow. Christian kept his vigil on
the sky, leading Sam upward and to the
right, to the west.

By some miracle that Samantha was never
able to fathom later, she found herself at the
top of a rise, leaning heavily upon Christian's arm, and below her, barely visible in
the thicket surrounding it, was a beautiful
clear rivulet of water that reflected the sun's
fading red-gold rays.

Samantha sat across from Christian, feeling better than she had in days. The tiny rivulet had quenched their thirst and had
miraculously replaced itself from a water

source that fed it before spilling over onto rocks and disappearing into the earth.

Handing Samantha a handkerchief that had been dipped in the water and wrung out, Christian smiled. "Tomorrow morning, we'll follow the direction of the water. It's my guess that farther up in the hills there's a wonderful spring, and perhaps even a little waterfall."

"You mean we might even be able to bathe?" Samantha asked hopefully.

"That's my bet."

When Sam fell asleep that night, before exhaustion overcame her, she dreamed of the spring and prayed for a waterfall.

In the morning, before the sun had barely skipped over the horizon, both Sam and Christian were eagerly on their way to discover the mother stream. There were times when the little river went underground and became difficult to follow. Other times, they could actually measure it growing in size.

Shortly after noon, they found it. Water. In all its glory. The sun danced over it, creating millions of shimmering lights in its dark blue depths. There was even the prayed-for waterfall, although it was only a few feet in height and was hardly more than a trickle.

"What did I tell you?" Christian laughed triumphantly. "The lady ordered a waterfall, and there it is."

"Somehow, I think I should have made my requirements more specific," Sam teased, already pulling off her shoes for the anticipated plunge into the shimmering pool.

Heedless of Christian's presence, she stripped down to her bra and bikini panties and leaped into the pool. The water was cool, actually cold, and took her breath away. After diving below the blue surface once again, she came up for air, giggling in delight.

"Do you sleep with your socks on, too?" Christian laughed, calling her attention to himself.

It was then that she saw he had already discarded his socks and boots, stripped off his shirt, and was unbuckling his pants.

"What are you doing?"

"Same as you, only with less."

Squealing with embarrassment, Samantha dove once again and came up on the far side of the pool. When she surfaced she saw that Christian was already up to his waist in the water, and the pile of clothing on the bank attested to the fact that he was naked.

"Why so embarrassed?" He laughed. "Listen, Orion, I'll make a deal with you. You wash my back and I'll wash yours."

"Ha! A likely story. You must think I'm pretty dumb to fall for a deal like that!"

Christian laughed. "Why not? Things got to be pretty nice between us out there on the desert. As a matter of fact, there were some nights there when you were pretty darned friendly."

Sam flushed. His manner was only half-teasing; his eyes were telling her something else altogether. "Christian, I expect you to behave like a gentleman. You keep to your side of the pool and I'll keep to mine."

"Talk about likely stories," he said, advancing on her. "More likely you'll take over fifty-one percent."

Staggering beneath the weight of his words, Samantha stepped backward. It had been so long since Christian had accused her of duping Gemini out of his inheritance that she had almost forgotten that the argument existed. The careless sting of his words and the decreasing distance Christian was putting between them sent a spur of panic into her chest. She stood, wading toward the far side of the pool where the water was more shallow. Beneath the sheer material of her bra, which was even more revealing when wet, Samantha's breasts were firm, and the rosy crests were erect from the coolness of the water. She saw Christian's eyes drift to them, his pleasure evidenced by his sultry look.

Still he advanced on her, closing the distance between them. In defense, not in play, she splashed him, heaving quantities of water at his head. He bent, grasping her knees, and pulled her down, the water closing over her head. Whooping for revenge, Samantha splashed and tormented him by threatening to run from the pool and steal his clothing. "Then see what kind of macho image you create running through the desert stark, staring naked!"

Laughing, Christian captured her and threatened to dip her under again. Screaming for mercy, Sam clung fiercely to him, her arms locked around his neck, her face pressed close to his.

Suddenly, it seemed as though time ceased to tick. Nothing, no one, existed in the whole world, only the two of them. Gently, he embraced her, cradling her head in one hand and supporting her back with the other. Backward, back, he dipped her and into her line of vision swept the sky and the scudding clouds. Slowly, deliberately, he bent his head, beads of water shining on his dark hair. Closer and closer his mouth came to hers.

Samantha gave her lips without reservation. She knew she would always give herself to this man, knowing with her whole heart and soul that he truly loved her. If only he would admit it—to her, to himself. She knew with that one, gentle kiss that she could never belong to another.

Christian lifted his head, questions in his silvery-gray eyes, his brows furled together over the bridge of his nose. He disengaged her arms from around his neck and stepped away from her.

"The water's getting cold," he growled, making her wonder if he was half as angry with her as he was with himself.

Late that afternoon, Samantha began to gather their freshly washed clothing from the surrounding bushes on which she had placed them to dry. She glanced over at Christian, who was busy gathering firewood with which to roast a small rabbit that he had successfully trapped earlier. When Sam had first seen the pathetic, limp little carcass before Christian skinned and dressed it, she swore she wouldn't touch a bite of it. Now, with her stomach complaining with hunger, she knew she would set her squeamishness aside.

As they had gone about their chores to make a comfortable camp for the night, there had been little communication between them. Christian seemed to be pondering his own thoughts and she was still remembering his remark about taking over of fifty-one percent of the pool. Money. Why did everything have to come down to money? *Gemini,* Sam said to herself, *you don't know what a curse that legacy has been. Why, for heaven's sake, did you do it? You must have had a reason, but for the life of me I can't think what it could have been.*

When the first stars were shining in the velvet-black sky, and the little fire was sputtering into glowing embers, Samantha rested against the rocks and patted her midsection. Much as she hated to admit it, the roasted rabbit was the best meal she could remember ever eating.

"I was afraid you'd be too squeamish to eat." The sudden sound of his voice in the still night startled her.

"Only my sensibilities are squeamish. My stomach had other ideas." She tried to keep her voice light while measuring his mood. There were times that to say Christian's moods were mercurial was an understatement.

"Orion, I've been thinking. Do you really mean what you say—that you never wanted and still don't want your inheritance of Delaney Enterprises?"

Sam's eyes widened. "Of course. I know I've never had a right to that inheritance. I still don't know why Gemini did that. It certainly had nothing to do with her feelings for you. She adored you; you know that.''

''Well, I've got my own ideas about Aunt Gemini. However, if you listened closely to the terms of the will, there's an addendum to be read in the near future. Also, it forbids you to either sell your shares or to sign them away.''

Now Sam's interest was definitely piqued. ''I remember something to that effect.''

''Now, before you go off the deep end, Orion, hear me out. If my calculations, and also my navigational skills, are correct, right over that ridge is California. If you're sincere about the inheritance, you'll marry me there. Community property laws would relieve you of twenty-five and one-half percent of Delaney Enterprises, still leaving you a rich woman, but putting the family business back into my control.''

Stunned, Samantha leaped to her feet. ''What are you trying to do? Test me? I've already told you I don't want it—*any* of it! Take it! Take it all!''

Christian's hands grabbed her arms painfully. "I can't take it, Orion. And you can't give it to me. You can't even sell it to me. This is the only way."

Samantha looked up into his face. There was a shadow in his eyes, a shadow she was certain wasn't created by the moonlight. There was an urgency in his voice she had never heard there before, and as the full reality of his proposal dawned on her, she thought her heart would break. Marry him? She would have cheerfully followed him to the end of the earth just to hear him say he loved her. Now, the thing she had wanted most ever since the first moment she had set her eyes on Christian Delaney had been made a mockery. A sham. Lowering her head so he couldn't read the pain in her eyes, she nodded, unable to hold back the biting words that she threw up in defense of her emotions. "As you say, I'd still be a rich woman. I'll go to sleep tonight dreaming of how I'll spend all that money—if we ever get out of this predicament alive, that is." Even to her own ears, her voice was dead sounding and unconvincing.

"Oh, we'll get out of this alive, all right," Christian said positively. "Come over here. I want to show you something." Unceremoniously, he led her to the top of the rise where he had been gathering firewood. Off in the distance, in the direction he was pointing, he told her to watch. After what seemed an endless moment, a sharp light appeared in the distance and swept across the horizon.

Not comprehending what she was seeing, Sam looked baffled.

"It's the highway, Orion. It's the road back to civilization!"

That night, while Christian slept, Samantha lay awake, huge silent tears dropping onto her cheeks.

Chapter Eight

Los Angeles Airport was a hub of confusion, and Samantha followed closely behind her new husband as they struggled through the crowd of businessmen and tourists. The confusion surrounding her was insignificant compared to the bewilderment she was feeling. So much had happened in the past three days that she believed she would never again gain a firm grip on reality.

Christian led her to a seat near Gate 53, where they would board their plane taking them back to Washington, D.C., and then murmured something about picking up a few magazines.

As he walked away, Samantha sat amidst the flurry of arrivals and departures as she reflected over the events that had led to her becoming Mrs. Christian Delaney. After trekking out of the hills and hitching a ride on the highway, they had found themselves in the little California town of Primo. While she had sat by, Christian had called the offices of *Daylight Magazine* and made several other quick phone calls. A quick shopping trip through Primo's minuscule business district and then a visit to the City Hall where they applied for their marriage license. Then Christian had taken her to the town's medical clinic, where she had stayed for rest and treatment from their desert ordeal. That was the last she had seen of Christian until he had checked her out of the clinic and then taken her to the magistrate's office, where they were married. Next was a chartered plane flight to Los Angeles and the airport.

A rapid machine-gun fire of events that were fuddled and baffling had brought her to the here and now. Mrs. Christian Delaney. A marriage of convenience. A marriage to prove that she wasn't the gold digger he accused her of being. A marriage that was a sham.

Aboard the jetliner that would take them back east, Samantha watched Christian and she saw that it wasn't until they were airborne that he relaxed. She hadn't realized just how uptight he had been. And he looked so tired. Drawn and fatigued. Suddenly, she wanted to cradle his head to her breast and whisper comforting words. She wanted to tell him she loved him and please not to contemplate divorce once they were back in Washington.

If sleep were the order of the day, she might as well do as Christian was doing. She slept fitfully, her dreams invaded by Christian Delaney chasing her across the desert. His sun-bronzed face was contorted in rage as he shouted angry words at her. Tripping and falling, she raced through the sand, screaming and yelling, begging him to believe her. *Let me explain!* she shouted over and over. *At least hear me out!* He was gaining on her, faster, faster. Her heart thundered as she fell in the sand, unable to get to her feet to escape him. *You don't understand. I had nothing to do with Gemini's will! I didn't even know about it. Listen to me! Why won't you believe me? Please, please love me!*

Samantha shuddered and woke up to see Christian leaning over her, a strange look on his weary face. "You were having a nightmare," he explained.

She felt disoriented, shaken, remembering the vivid dream. Had she cried out? "I'm sorry if I woke you up," she said quietly, trying to fathom the expression in his eyes.

"You didn't wake me up. Are you all right now?"

Was that concern she heard in his voice? Instead of answering him, she closed her eyes again, feigning sleep. From beneath her heavily fringed lashes, she watched as he settled himself in the seat. She had never actually seen a man's shoulders slump before, indicative of defeat. She must be wrong, she told herself. It was merely fatigue. Men like Christian Delaney were never defeated.

Now that she was married, her life was bound to be different somehow. Even though her marriage would never be consummated. Even though it would quickly end with divorce. When they arrived back in Washington, she would go her way and he would go his. Lawyers would handle everything. There would be no chance meetings, no pounding hearts, no tears for what might have been.

In the *Daylight Magazine* offices the marriage between Christian Delaney and resident photographer Orion was completely misinterpreted and met with overwhelming good wishes and congratulatory handshakes. Neither Christian nor Samantha explained that the real reason behind the marriage was to relieve Samantha of the twenty-five and one-half percent of Delaney stock in order to return a controlling interest to the publisher.

Sam deduced that Christian must have made the announcement of their nuptials by phone from California because Lizzy and

Charlie seemed to have planned the whole shebang. There were canapés and champagne and well wishes all around. When a toast was made to the new bride and groom, Christian pleased his staff by planting a kiss on Samantha's lips.

It was with relief that Sam noticed Charlie pull Christian away from the festivities on urgent office business. Seizing the opportunity to escape the festivities, Sam gathered up her camera case and slung it over her shoulder. It was time to go home. She frowned. Where exactly was home? Home was the basement apartment next door to Gemini's where she paid the rent. And then she must make arrangements to have the cats returned to her. They were, after all, still her responsibility until the respective attorneys settled the question of their custody.

Sam laid the camera case on the nearest chair. How could she have forgotten? Christian Delaney said she was fired. That meant she had to clean out her desk and take her belongings with her. She might as well do it now and be done with it. This way she wouldn't have to make another trip back to the office and chance a stray meeting with her publisher husband. It would be clean and quick. Forget all those brave, indignant things she had said and thought about on the long plane ride home. If he didn't want her working for his company, she wouldn't. The day would never come when she would force herself on an employer or a man. The fifty-one percent could rot for all she cared. For now, all she wanted was to pick up the pieces of her life and get on with it the best way she knew how.

Her task took all of ten minutes. She would have to hurry or the taxi would leave without her. Two manila envelopes full of pictures, a spare makeup case, and her camera under her arms, she left the tiny cubbyhole that had been her short-lived office. She didn't look back; she couldn't.

Inside her own small apartment she very carefully locked the door, shot the dead bolt, and then slid the chain into place. Even a SWAT team couldn't break down this door with its grille over the paned glass. She was safe. But who was she safe from? Christian Delaney?

Sam walked around the small apartment, touching this and that. Her personal things that she had left behind held meaning only for her. Something was bothering her, and then it hit full force. She really was stupid. Coming back to this apartment was the most stupid thing she could have done. Hadn't he told her that he was taking over Gemini's apartment? Right now, this very minute, he could be upstairs. Her heart began its wild fluttering. Why had she done such a stupid thing? *Because,* a niggling voice said quietly, subconsciously, *you knew he would be there and you wanted to be as close to him as possible.*

Dejectedly, Sam sat down on the sofa and let the tears flow. It was true. She did want to be near Christian, in the hopes that he would come to her and say the past was past and he did truly love her. Would she ever hear him say those words to her?

Panicking with the turn her thoughts were taking, Sam looked around for something to do. The cats. A quick call placed to the vet's and the cats would find their way home in a taxi. Then a shower—a long, cold shower. And an aspirin. Two of them!

An hour later the cats, Gin and Tonic, were stretched out under the cocktail table. "I really feel sorry for you guys, the way you've been shifted from pillar to post. I have some chicken livers in the freezer along with a few gizzards. And I'm going to cook them for you right now. Now that I'm a married lady, I suddenly feel very domestic." Gin nipped at Tonic, who, in turn, snarled his revenge by way of a clout with his paw on Gin's head. Gin's back arched and he spat his anger, which Tonic ignored. "Go to it, guys. Get it out of your system, because you aren't getting high on me. This is a dry house as far as you're concerned."

Sam added a few onions and a little salt and pepper to the livers and gizzards and decided they would be wasted on the cats; besides, she was hungry herself. She quickly plucked a package of cat food from beneath the sink and filled two small bowls. She poured milk into a medium-sized dish and added a drop of rum flavoring as an inducement and then whistled for the cats. As always, they ignored her. "So starve," she muttered, spooning the chicken livers and gizzards onto a dinner plate.

The hours crawled by, and to Sam's disgust there was no visit or even a phone call from Christian Delaney. The least he could have done was make some sort of overture so she could reject him. This should have been her honeymoon. She was spending her honeymoon with two reformed alcoholic cats. "This is the pits," she snapped at the cats as she crawled into bed.

The first thing she did the following morning was call the Women's Bank to ask an officer to recommend a woman attorney. She scribbled down the number and called for an appointment. She circled a date a week into the future and then stared at the calendar.

She should start thinking about her future and what she was going to do. Should she take a trip to the unemployment office? Was she fired or had she quit? And what about the name change? Already she was getting a headache and it was only midmorning. She had to do something constructive like shower and dress. Then she'd make a trip to the market for some food and stop at the post office to pick up her mail. She would buy a few newspapers and see what the job market was offering for unemployed photographers. That should take care of her time till early afternoon. Then she could do some laundry, prepare a little dinner, watch some television, and go to bed. "Some honeymoon," she grimaced. Was she really legally married?

Sam completed her errands and was back in front of the television screen in time to catch the four-thirty movie. A Chinese TV dinner was heating in the oven. The cats were napping contentedly. She kicked off her shoes and propped her slim ankles on the edge of the cocktail table as she sorted through the mail. A sale flyer from Woody's, an American Express bill, the utility bill, scads of letters addressed to Occupant or Resident, and a legal-looking letter from Gemini's lawyer. The most important first. She decided she could live with owing American Express $123.46. She would have to pass up Woody's sale and

write out a check for the utility company or
have her power cut off. The stiff, crackling,
legal paper informed her that she was to be
in the attorney's office on Monday, the seventeenth, for the reading of the addendum to
Gemini's will. The meeting was to take place
at ten-thirty in the morning. Did she have to
go? Probably not, she answered herself. After all, she was engaging her own attorney to
handle matters. Still, perhaps she should go
so that when she met with her private lawyer
she would have more knowledge about the
current state of affairs. She would go and
demand copies of everything in triplicate.
Gemini had always said to get everything in
triplicate. They can fool you once, even
twice, but three times? That was another
story. She wouldn't sign anything unless it
was in triplicate.

Sam stared at the sleeping cats and then
her eye fell on the silent phone. Why
couldn't it ring? Why couldn't Christian call
her to see if she was all right? New hus-
bands shouldn't be so…blasé about…about
their wives.

The timer on the stove buzzed. The TV dinner was done. She peeled back the foil from the tray and stared at the messy-looking concoction. Yuk! She couldn't eat this... this mess. She had to eat something. The refrigerator yielded little in the way of food: a mushy apple, some cheese that was stiff and hard around the edges, and some grape jam. She should have bought real food when she stopped by the neighborhood deli. A stale breadstick in the breadbox did nothing to enhance her appetite. She was back to square one and the TV dinner. Morosely, she picked at the steamy, stringy chow mein and chewed on the barely visible rubbery shrimp.

It took her less than five minutes to straighten out the kitchen and replenish the cats' dishes with canned milk. Listlessly, she walked back to the living room and the noisy television. Whatever Woody Allen was doing, it must be funny. She decided if the Allen movie couldn't distract her, nothing could. Irritably, she switched off the set.

Time was laying heavily on her hands. Samantha needed to interest herself in something, yet she admitted that she found she would pause, stand stock-still, and listen for some movement upstairs—footsteps, the clatter of a pot, something that would tell her Christian was upstairs in Gemini's apartment. She fully realized the need to feel close to him.

As she wandered through her apartment, she entered the spare bedroom where she had spent so many hours working on Christian's portrait. She would probably never finish it now. How could she? Every line of his face had become dear to her. She would have tried to breathe life into that painting, wishing it could become the man she had come to know so well.

Her lazy gaze fell on the camera and gadget bag, the same ones she had carried through the desert. Suddenly spurred to action, she hefted the bag and carried it to the portion of the spare bedroom off the bathroom where she had set up a darkroom. Her blood tingled and her interest sparked. The film, the pictures that she and Christian had snapped of one another throughout their time in the Southwest.

Working quickly, but deftly and untiringly, she developed the twelve rolls of film that held the memories and images of those seemingly long-ago days when Christian had been within reach of her fingertips.

The long strips of positives and negatives hung from a makeshift clothesline to dry. Finally, admitting her exhaustion, she crept to her bed, to sleep, to dream, to relive her adventure with the man she loved. She had worked blindly, her hands going through the motions. She hadn't dared to pause and dwell on the pictures developing before her eyes. She had to sleep, and that wouldn't be possible if she studied the photographs. The memory was too fresh, too new. Soon, hopefully, she would be strong enough to look at them, cherish them. But for now, she would escape her pain and sleep.

When the phone rang shortly after noon the next day, it sounded like an alarm. Sam stared at the phone a moment before she realized it wasn't ringing. The alarming sound had been the doorbell. Was it Christian? If it was, what was she going to say to him? What was there to say? Nothing, she grimaced as she released the chain and slid the dead bolt. Before she opened the door, she asked, "Who is it?"

"Barbara Matthews from the *Post*. I'd like to talk to you, Mrs. Delaney."

Mrs. Delaney! She was Mrs. Delaney. "Why?" Sam demanded through the door.

"I think my readers might be interested in your new marriage to one of the most eligible bachelors in the country. I want to do it for the Sunday section. I'll only take up an hour of your time."

How could she refuse? She knew how hard journalists worked and how difficult it was sometimes to fill space. Why not? What did she have to lose? Sam opened the door to admit a vivacious, sparkling redhead who was at first glance a sizzling size three. Sam hated her on sight. "Come in," she said graciously. She motioned for the petite reporter to sit on the sofa and then sat down across from her in a shabby leather chair.

Barbara settled herself comfortably and flipped her notebook to a clean page. "I'll ask the questions, and if you have something you want to interject, feel free to interrupt me. First of all," she said in a lilting, musical voice, "tell me, how does it feel to be Mrs. Christian Delaney?"

This was a mistake. She must have been out of her mind to agree to this interview. "Well...I...it's..."

"There's no way to describe it, right?" Barbara said, making squiggly marks on her pad. "My readers will understand that. All that money! You'll be able to go anywhere, do anything. How have you handled that?"

What's to handle? Sam thought huffily. "I personally think...actually...you see..."

"It's mind-boggling. I understand, and my readers will certainly relate to that. Wishful thinking, if you know what I mean. How do you think you'll like having servants to wait on you and cater to your every need? You *were* a working girl like the rest of us."

"I've always been...been rather in-independent and..."

"You'll handle it like you were born to it, right? Good, good answer; my readers will identify. Now, tell me," Barbara said, leaning over and whispering confidentially, "is he as romantic as the tabloids make him out to be? Does he really have steely eyes that can cut you to ribbons, or do they go all soft and melting, making your head swoon?''

"That's . . . that's a . . . a fair . . .''

"I knew I was right, I just knew it!'' Barbara chortled, making a quick row of scratches on her pad. "He'd make a perfect Adonis!'' she all but squealed. "Gifts. Has your new husband showered you with gifts yet?''

"Well, actually . . . you see, it's been such a short . . . what I mean is . . .''

"You don't have to say another word. I understand perfectly. He'll do the showering when you leave for your honeymoon. By the way, where is that to take place?'' the reporter inquired.

Would the reporter believe her if she told her she was honeymooning alone? Not likely. Sam flushed a bright crimson. "I don't think Chris . . . Listen, you don't understand. I really shouldn't be talking to you. You've got it all wrong . . .''

"But of course, I understand. It's a secret, right? I don't blame you for one minute. It's just that my poor readers are so starved for romance that they eat this sort of thing right up and beg for more. I'm sure a round-the-world cruise is not out of the question, right?"

"Right," Sam squealed. She had to get this girl out of here before she suffered a nervous breakdown.

Barbara Matthews coughed to clear her throat. Holding her hand over her mouth, she complained, "Too much talking. Gets me right here." She coughed again.

"Can I offer you something? A drink? Coffee?"

"I would like a drink if you don't mind. Bourbon, straight up," she said firmly.

That was good. No ice in the drink. The cats would continue to sleep. Once they heard the clink of ice or the opening of a bottle, it would be all over. Deftly, Sam poured the bourbon into a squat glass, one eye on the snoozing cats. She extended the drink to her guest and let her breath out in a deep sigh. The cats hadn't noticed.

The petite Miss Matthews downed her drink neatly and immediately asked another question. "Now, Mrs. Delaney, for the record and for my more liberated readers, tell me what you're going to do about your job. Do you plan to continue with your work, or are you going to become, how shall I say it"—she pursed her mouth, seeking the right word and finally came up with it—"domesticated?"

I wonder what she would think if I told her I'm applying for unemployment compensation tomorrow? Sam mused. "I haven't decided exactly...I think what I'll do is..."

"Play the housewife bit for a while. Perfectly understandable. I'd do the same thing myself. Children...what about children? Do you see any in your immediate future?"

Sam's neck was beginning to perspire. "At least a dozen," she said bluntly.

Barbara Matthews scribbled furiously. "Mrs. Delaney, when can I meet Mr. Delaney? I would like a few good quotes from him. I guess he isn't home from the office yet. I really have to get back to my paper and get started on this. Listen, what do you say we fudge a little?"

Sam blinked, not quite understanding what the reporter meant.

Barbara Matthews continued. "What I mean is, if I were to ask Mr. Delaney if he was madly in love with you, he would naturally say yes, right? And if I asked him if he was going to show you the world and shower you with presents, he'd tell me yes to that, too. So, why don't I just say that and this way I won't have to hang around and wait for him and spoil your evening? By the way, why are you still here? Oh, never mind. I know, you're getting a few things together. Sometimes," she said, throwing her hands in the air, "I get so flighty, I don't know what I'm doing. But don't you worry about a thing. I'm really going to knock myself out on this interview. Did you by any chance see the piece I did on the two pandas at the zoo?"

"No, I guess I missed it," Sam said defensively.

"Not to worry. I'll send you a copy. Say, would you mind if I used your powder room?"

"No...no...it's right through there." Sam pointed. Anything, anything at all to be rid of this woman.

Barbara Matthews went into the bathroom through the spare bedroom and Sam tapped her fingertips impatiently on the arm of the chair. Her eye fell on the empty glass that had held the bourbon the reporter had downed in one gulp. Quickly, she picked up the glass and brought it out to the kitchen before the girl could suggest another drink to whet her whistle. Sam wanted Miss Matthews out of her apartment—as soon as possible!

When Sam returned to the living room, she had expected to find the reporter waiting for her. Instead, after a few minutes, Miss Matthews exited from the spare bedroom. Somehow, imperceptibly, her attitude was altered.

"Thank you so much for your time, Mrs. Delaney." She winked slyly. "I do so envy you. You really did snare yourself some hunk. Every woman in the country is going to hate you with a passion for taking Christian Delaney out of circulation." If anything, Barbara Matthews' speech was even more rapid than before. For some reason, Sam felt that the reporter wanted to leave the apartment even more desperately than she wanted to be rid of her.

"Don't you worry about being envied, Mrs. Delaney," the reporter chattered while she slipped into her coat. "You just take it in your stride. Once the women of America get to know you as I have, they'll all take you to their hearts. 'Poor little working girl marries super-rich tycoon.' I'm going to do a fabulous piece of work on this one. Thanks again and much happiness." The girl literally lunged for the door. In the space of an instant, she was gone.

Samantha leaned against the door. What in the world was going on here? A dizzy reporter from the *Post* shows up and harasses her into an interview and then takes off out of the apartment as though the hounds of hell were on her heels.

Chapter Nine

Three days passed without Christian Delaney getting in touch with her. Sam sat down on the couch, her mind racing. Today was Sunday; tomorrow was the reading of the addendum to the will. Today was also the day the article Barbara Matthews was working on would appear in the special section of the Sunday paper.

Sam glanced at her watch. She had all day to get through before her meeting tomorrow at the attorney's office. Tomorrow she would see Christian. Still, she had to get through the rest of the day. The zoo! She would go to the zoo and see the pandas herself. She would stop at the deli and ask them to pack her up a picnic lunch, and she would spend the day wandering around the zoo. No decisions to be made today. Tomorrow it would be all over.

Donning warm clothing, Sam left the apartment, stopping at the deli for her lunch and a copy of the Sunday paper. Her eye fell on the left hand corner of the newspaper and a square box with a Santa climbing down a chimney. It was a reminder that there were only eight more shopping days till Christmas. Sam was appalled. Eight days! Where had the time gone?

Her purchases intact, Sam left the corner store and walked up Woodley Road on her way to the zoo.

She tramped through the zoo, getting colder by the minute. Lately, it seemed that all she did was make mistakes. She really didn't feel like roaming around looking at animals in cages. She admitted that the steamy, smelly birdhouse would do nothing for her except possibly curb her appetite. It was only three-thirty, but it would be dark soon. And if she wasn't mistaken, it felt like snow. A sudden wind whipped up, blowing her coat collar high around her neck. Sam clutched at it and buttoned the toggle securely and huddled down into the warmth the heavy coat provided. She wished she had a hat, something to keep her ears warm.

Sam started the uphill climb to the exit, holding on to the iron rail. She raised her head slightly as she felt something wet hit her nose. It was snowing. How she loved the first snowfall of the year! She might as well go home now. She hitched the heavy Sunday paper and her paper bag, holding the lunch she hadn't gotten around to eating, more firmly under her arm. Small children laughing and giggling raced ahead of her as the giant clock at the entrance sounded the time. She smiled as she listened to the tune. The wind was stronger now and the snow seemed to be falling a bit more heavily. She was surprised to see a soft carpet of the white stuff covering the ground already. And she had been oblivious to it all afternoon. It certainly didn't say much for her state of mind.

Inside her snug apartment Sam dropped the soggy Sunday newspaper onto the cocktail table and removed her coat. She'd make herself some soup and have crackers with it for dinner, take a warm bath, and then read the paper. After that she would sort out her thoughts and make plans for what she was going to do with the rest of her life after her visit to Gemini's lawyer tomorrow. There were no two ways about it; she had to get on with her life, without or with Christian Delaney.

Her light dinner finished, her bath completed, Sam powdered herself lavishly with Esther's last birthday present to her—Zen bath powder. She wrinkled her nose appreciatively; she loved the sweet, intoxicating scent. She slipped into a scarlet velour robe and tied the sash.

Wind whistled outside the grilled windows and Sam shivered. The small bedroom was drafty. Her eyes traveled to the freestanding fireplace in the corner of the bedroom, the main reason she had rented the apartment from Gemini. A quick-burning Duraflame log and she was set. Was it her imagination, or did she feel warmer already? Power of suggestion, she mused.

Settling herself comfortably beneath the floral comforter, Sam snuggled back against a mound of pillows. She felt rather like a bird in a nest. Deftly, she tossed aside the first three sections of the heavy, wet newspaper and searched for Barbara Matthews' article. She found it on page two of the Living section.

What she saw shocked her as though she'd stuck her finger in an electrical socket. Pictures! Her pictures! The pictures she and Christian had taken of one another with her father's Hasselblad during their trek in the desert!

Throwing back the comforter, stumbling on it as it caught around her legs, she leaped for the spare bedroom. Those were *her* pictures! The ones she had developed and had left hanging from the clothesline in the darkroom. How... how had Barbara Matthews gotten her hands on them?

Switching on the light in the spare bedroom, her eyes first fell on the easel holding Christian's portrait and saw it was still covered with the paint-stained old sheet she had thrown over it. Almost fearfully, hoping against hope, she looked toward the end of the room where she had created the darkroom. The long strips of negatives still hung there, but the positives were gone. And she knew who had taken them!

"No, no, no!" she heard herself cry aloud as she rushed over to them. Quickly examining them, she saw with her own eyes the figures in the negatives were one and the same with the pictures in the Sunday paper.

Her mind snapped back to Barbara Matthews' visit. The reporter must have taken them when Samantha had allowed her to use the bathroom. That was why she had seemed in such a hurry to get out of the apartment.

Samantha felt her knees buckle under her. It was a dirty, low-down trick. But there was no help for it now. The damage had been done. Christian would either see the article or, at the very least, hear about it. Whatever, the end result would be the same. He would think she had maliciously offered the snapshots to the reporter, and he would hate her with a passion!

In a flurry of panic, Samantha rushed back to where she had dropped the paper. She was compelled to read it, to examine the photos. Somewhere in the article they would have to give credit for the photos. Somehow, she felt she couldn't believe what was happening to her until she saw her name in print. It was just a bad dream, she repeated over and over in her mind.

Diving for the paper, her eyes tried to take it all in at once. Disciplining her attention, she slowed and looked more carefully. Christian would think she had selected them to make him appear foolish. There was one of him looking over his shoulder at the camera, a silly wink and a silly smile on his face. Another taken by an outcropping of rocks . . . sitting beside the campfire . . . and one in which they had used the delayed timing and both were in the shot together, sitting close, the campfire casting shadows and light on their features and making them look incredibly romantic. There were eleven photos, each more compromising than the one before.

Sam's eyes raked the column of print. It appeared the reporter was big on pictures and small on words. Sam's eyes widened as she read the text and she gasped. She had said no such things!

Good heavens! Where had the reporter gotten such an idea? This was beyond belief! People were actually going to read this and believe it! Correction: it was an early edition of the paper; people had already read it. Christian must have seen it. Oh, no! She whimpered into the pillow. She would sue; that's what she would do, the first thing in the morning. It must be libelous; it had to be. She hadn't said anything like this. Where did that stupid reporter get such ideas? She would never be able to face Christian Delaney again. This couldn't be happening to her; it just couldn't. A bright flush stained her fresh-scrubbed face. Even her ears felt hot. She felt ashamed, mortified, and darned indignant. Tears welled in her eyes at her predicament. Now, what was she going to do?

The blue-white flame from the fireplace blurred her vision as she stared into the flickering flames. She had to do something about a rebuttal. A letter—she would write a letter to the paper and one to Christian Delaney denying... denying what? She had to get her thoughts together and think this through, and she had to do it before the meeting tomorrow morning.

Sam tossed back the covers and walked over to the shuttered window. She opened the louvers and stared at the whiteness beyond the pane of glass. It looked like a winter wonderland in the mellow glow of the streetlight. The wind was strong and she could hear it shrieking in the trees near the curb as the branches dripped and swayed with their mantle of whiteness. It had been a long time since she had seen snow like this in Washington. It would be a white Christmas, after all. The thought depressed her.

The slim girl shivered in the draft from the window. She closed the louvers and looked longingly at the warm bed she had just left. A cup of tea would do her good right now, she decided, and she really should also

change the litter box. It would give her
something to do while she thought about the
interview in the Sunday paper.

Sam had just tossed the tea bag into the
trash container when the doorbell sounded.
She frowned and looked at the kitchen
clock. It was eight-fifty. Who could be vis-
iting her on such a night? She walked hesitantly to the front door and peeked through
the tiny peephole. Christian Delaney! Sam
swallowed hard. What did he want? The
doorbell chimed a second time. He had read
the paper! Oh, no! She swallowed again and
released the chain. Her shaking hands slid
the dead bolt and then the regular lock. She
moistened her dry lips and swung open the
door, her face impassive. ''Yes?'' she asked
quietly.

''May I come in? It's rather blustery out
here, as you can see.'' Sam said nothing but
stood aside for him to enter. She watched as
he shook the snow from his tweed jacket and
brushed at his hair. She was surprised that he
wore no overcoat, then remembered that he
only had to come from as far away as next
door, which meant walking down two flights

of stairs. She closed the door but made no move toward the living room. She waited, her heart pounding in her chest. Suddenly, she was aware, acutely aware, of her shiny scrubbed face with its layer of cold cream and even more acutely aware of her naked body beneath the scarlet robe.

Christian Delaney stared at her and then walked into the living room. She had to follow him if she wanted to find out what he wanted. She waited till he sat down on the sofa and then she perched herself on the arm of the wing chair across from him. Still, she said nothing, waiting to see why he was here.

"I came to congratulate you on the article in the *Post*. I had no idea that you were so...so articulate or that you cared so much." Sam felt a chill wash over her at the sarcastic tone. Would he believe her if she explained? And why did she have to explain? Let him believe whatever he wanted. She shrugged and remained mute. Christian frowned.

"Did you read the article?" he asked nonchalantly. Sam nodded. "I was more than a little surprised to see the photographs. Somehow, I hadn't expected you would sell them to the *Post*. *Time* would have been my guess." His voice was quiet, dangerously quiet, and his face betrayed no hint of what he was truly feeling. If anything, he seemed faintly amused.

"I . . . I didn't sell them . . ."

"No? Foolish girl. *Time* would have paid you a small fortune for them. Oh, that's right, I almost forgot." He snapped his fingers. "You don't need money, do you? Not with what Aunt Gemini left you. So, why did you do it? Spite?"

"No, you don't understand. I developed those photos the other night, and when that reporter asked to use the bathroom . . . Oh, what's the use? You'll never believe she stole them."

"Try me," he said, a strange, soft note coming into his voice. His silvery gaze penetrated her, beseeching her to make him believe her.

"It's just as I told you. I let her use the bathroom. She went in through the spare bedroom. I never thought . . ." Samantha drew herself to full height and squared her shoulders. "Barbara Matthews *stole* those photos from this apartment! That is the truth. I would never, could never, be so low-down as to publish them. They were ours, Christian." A sob rose in her throat. "They belonged to us, and I'm angrier than a hornet to think that they've been made public!"

Christian moved close to her, making her dizzy with his mere presence. "At one time in the desert you threatened to publish the photos."

"I'd never do it. It was only a threat. I wanted to rile you."

"That you did, most successfully." A slow smile crept onto his face, softening his features and bringing humor to his mysterious silver-gray eyes. "The one I liked best was the one of you with your shirt wrapped around your head. And that silly one of you washing our clothes in the spring like an old Indian woman." He laughed, relaxing, believing her.

"It would be nice if you offered me a drink—a celebration, so to speak."

If she fixed him a drink, she would have to move, and she knew her shaking legs and trembling hands would give away her emotions. "Help yourself," she said, motioning to the small cabinet holding the liquor. Christian stared at her a moment, then rose to make his own drink. He carried a bottle of liquor and a glass to the cocktail table and set them down. He frowned a second time as he removed the cap from the vodka and poured a drink. "Ice would be nice," he said quietly.

Sam blinked. Both cats were on the cocktail table in a second, clawing and spitting in their quest for the liquor. "Stop them!" Sam screeched. "Don't let them have any liquor! I'm drying them out!" Feverishly, she reached for Gin, who leaped out of her way and landed on Christian's lap, clawing at his jacket. "Now, look what you've done!" Sam cried as she tried to wipe up the spilled liquor with the hem of her robe, revealing a shapely, satiny leg and thigh.

"What the...?" Christian sputtered as he saw the vodka bottle topple as Gin fought Tonic for the aromatic spirits.

"Do you know what you just did? Why couldn't you pour the drink over the cabinet? Oh, no, you had to bring it over here, and now see what happened? I've had those cats on the wagon for a long time, and you just undid all my good work. Well, they're your responsibility now, and you can just take them with you when you leave here. They're all yours," Sam said angrily.

"The least you could do is help me clean it up." Frantically, she ran to the kitchen for a dish cloth and tried to wipe up the spilled liquor. Once her eyes met Christian's as she mopped at the table. The scarlet robe had parted and an expanse of creamy bosom was visible to his sleepy, silvery gaze. Hastily, she dropped the cloth and drew the robe tighter around her. A dull flush worked its way up her throat and into her cheeks.

"I'm sorry," Christian said huskily. "I had no idea the cats were still boozing it up. You should have warned me. I can see now that we have to do something about them."

"Not we! You have to do something about them! I'm giving them back to you—now!" Deftly, she scooped up the drunken cats and placed them in their basket. "Here's your cats and there's the door."

Christian grinned. "Would you really turn me and those poor, defenseless cats out on a night like this? According to that article I read today, you are a hopeless romantic. I refuse to leave!" he said adamantly.

"Well, you aren't staying here," Sam shot back.

"Of course I am. We're married, and those cats are both our responsibilities. I think," he said, grinning widely, "the best thing to do right now is let them sleep it off, and we should turn in ourselves."

Sam blanched. "As far as *I'm* concerned, we're not married! The whole idea was to legally transfer the Delaney stock to you. A marriage of convenience."

"You told the whole world, via the *Post*, that we were married and wanted dozens of children. I'm here to make that wish come true. In the eyes of the *Washington Post*, we're married, and that's good enough for me," he said in an amused voice. "Are you ready?"

Sam pretended ignorance. "Ready for what?" As if she didn't know. One moment she was spitting and hissing at him with her eyes, and the next she was pinned in his strong arms. He held her firmly, diminishing her struggles and overpowering her gasped objections. His lips were on the soft skin beneath her ear; his face was buried in the soft curls that clung to her neck. Insistent, persuasive, his mouth explored her skin, finding and pursuing the pleasure points that sent shudders through her body and made her weak. In spite of herself, Samantha clung to him, relishing this one heady moment, expecting it to be ripped away from her, leaving her bereft and alone and missing him.

Tenderly, he held her head in his hands, lifting her face for his kiss, touching her lips with his in a way that was both familiar and exciting. His hands traveled the length of her body, molding it and pressing it closer to his. She strained toward him, allowing him to hold her this way, loving it, loving him. Softly, so softly that at first she thought she imagined it, his voice rumbled deep in his chest and he whispered her name, "Samantha." A whisper so soft, so poignant, it fed the fires of her desire and echoed in her heart. Again, he whispered her name, telling her the things that lovers say, whispering them for her, words she had given up all hope of ever hearing from Christian.

He gathered her up in his arms, carrying her to the bedroom, taking her from the light into the dark, taking her with him into a world filled with the sound of his voice and the feel of his arms. A safe world, a place where his arms sheltered her and his lips worshipped her. Together they tumbled down the endless corridors created by their love. Together they found the hidden springs of their desires and the gardens of trust and belonging.

Christian was tender; he was forceful. He was all things for all times, and she responded to him, loving him, knowing that he loved her. He made her his own; he turned back the pages of her girlhood and introduced her to the fulfilled future of a woman. And always, he loved her.

For a thousand times his lips touched hers. For an eternity his hands possessed her. He touched her body and evoked an answering cry in her soul. Her heart belonged to Christian, for now, forever. And later, a short eternity later, when the fire had died down to low embers and lit the room with a faint orange glow, it was Christian who looked down at her with wonder in his eyes, softening their silvery hardness to molten pewter. And when he spoke, it was to whisper her name.

Chapter Ten

Sam woke up slowly, a feeling of contentment in every pore of her body. A slow, happy smile worked its way around the corners of her mouth. It wasn't a dream. It had been real, every single minute of the long night. She stretched luxuriously, deliberately postponing the moment when she would open her eyes and then touch her husband, lying beside her. She wanted to savor each second until she could no longer struggle against the need to feel his warm, hard body against hers. She couldn't stand

it another moment. Squeezing her eyes
tighter, she reached out and groped beneath
the covers. A sinking feeling settled in her
stomach. He was gone! "Christian!" she
cried softly, thinking he was in the bathroom. There was no answer.

A sob gathered in her throat as she rolled
over on the bed and pummeled the pillows
with clenched hands. He was gone. How
could he do this to her? How could he go off
and leave her without saying something?
Anything, even a goodbye, would be better
than waking up with this cold, dead feeling.
"I hate him! I hate him!" she cried, over
and over, as tears soaked the pillow beneath
her face, feeling used and foolish.

Crying and making herself sick wasn't
going to help. She had to get up and shower.
A note. Perhaps he didn't want to wake her
up and had left a note. He was considerate.
Surely, he had left a note. There was nothing.

Her tears long dried, she sat on the sofa,
and it wasn't until both cats staggered to the
cocktail table and began licking at the sticky
surface that anger rose in her, threatening to

choke the life from her body. He had left the cats! Just who did he think he was, barging into her apartment and giving the cats liquor and plying her with soft words and taking her to bed to exercise his matrimonial rights? And she had let him! What a fool she was! Now, she had to go to the lawyer's office and face him.

Sam managed somehow to get through her morning ritual of showering and dressing by habit. Everything she did was automatic, with no thought beyond the moment and what she was doing.

Opening the drapes, she was stunned to see the monstrous accumulation of snow that greeted her gaze. It was a known fact that the District of Columbia fell apart when snow had the audacity to accumulate more than an inch. This looked to her unpracticed eyes like a good eight inches. There would be no buses, and cabs would be at a premium. If she wanted to reach the lawyer's office, she would have to walk. And she would have to start out as soon as possible if she wanted to make the appointment any way near on time.

Sam rummaged in her closet for a heavy sheepskin jacket and also dug out a fur-lined hat from a box in the corner. Bright orange mittens, a gift from Norma Jean back in college days, completed her outfit. She looked down at her serviceable boots and prayed that the manufacturer's label proclaiming them to be waterproof was accurate.

If she hadn't been so miserable, she would have enjoyed her trek to the lawyer's office. People were scattered everywhere, cheerfully digging out cars and helping one another as playful children pelted one and all with snowballs that dissolved on impact. She trudged on, dodging the flying snowballs, careful to watch her footing. If there was one thing she didn't need, it was a broken bone of any kind.

Exactly one hour and forty minutes later she stomped her way into the lobby of the law offices. The blast of warm air made her blink and wish she was back outside in the clear brisk air. Shaking the snow from her jacket, she walked to the elevator and waited.

The ferns were still intact, as was the smell of lemon polish on the furniture. It was still as dry and dusty as before. Sam wrinkled her nose, fighting off a sneeze. She looked around and was surprised to see a handsome young man advance in her direction. He held out his hand and smiled. "David Carpenter. You must be Samantha Blakely. Follow me. I'll be conducting this meeting. Your aunt's attorney, my uncle, is home in bed with the flu. I'm a junior partner of the firm. I hope you don't have any objections to my handling the affairs."

"Of course not," Sam muttered as she followed David Carpenter's long-legged stride down the corridor. Anything was an improvement over Gemini's age-old friend.

While the young attorney gathered his papers together, Sam looked around the office and liked what she saw. The brown and beige plaid drapes were partially closed to ward off the intense glare from the white world outside. The low-slung beige leather chairs were comfortable and matched the thick pile of the cocoa carpeting. It was a room whose atmosphere was restful and masculine. The rich pecan of the paneled walls reminded Sam of Gemini's library, as did the copper bowls full of daisies and ferns. Her inspection of the room completed, Sam turned her gaze to the lawyer and waited for him to speak.

David Carpenter cleared his throat and then leaned back in his swivel chair. "Back there in the hallway I referred to you as Samantha Blakely. I apologize. I should have called you by your newly married name, Mrs. Delaney. It's just that I've been working on this case for so long, and Sam Blakely has become engraved on my brain. In the beginning I made the same mistake my uncle made in thinking you were a man. Your husband, as you know, was most upset. However, rest assured that he and I both spent several hours this morning going over matters, and he understands his Aunt Gemini's intentions."

"Mr. Carpenter, where is . . . my . . . hus— . . . Where is Christian?" Sam asked hesitantly.

"He left here thirty minutes ago. He said he had pressing business at the office. He left a message for you, though. Now, let me see, where did I put it? Oh, yes, here it is. 'I'll be home for dinner, and make my steak rare.'"

Sam's heart soared and took wing. Christian would be home for dinner! She was going to cook for him, and he liked his steak rare. Her smile, when she turned it on the young attorney, was as dazzling as the brightness outside the plaid-covered windows. "Thank you for telling me."

"No problem. Now, let me see. Yes, here it is. This is a letter addressed to you, written by Gemini Delaney shortly before her death. You were only to receive it if you were married to Mr. Delaney. Otherwise, it was to be destroyed." Rifling through his papers, he withdrew an envelope that was addressed to Mrs. Samantha Delaney.

Sam extended her shaking fingers to accept the stiff bond paper. Seeing Gemini's scratchy handwriting renewed a pang of grief. Fighting back tears, she forced herself to open the envelope and read Gemini's last message to her:

Dearest Samantha,
    Forgive an old woman's meddling,

but the very fact you are reading this letter means my nasty little scheme has ended with you being married to my nephew, Christian. Let it suffice to say that the end has justified the means.

I have made no secret of my deepest regard for you or of my loving fondness for Christian. My problem was in seeing the two of you find each other. I knew you were the girl for him from the moment I set eyes on you. The difficulty existed in having Christian discover this for himself.

It was a simple matter of having him notice you, and I could think of no better way of assuring this than having him think you were the beneficiary of the controlling interest in Delaney Enterprises. I'll bet *that* made him sit up and take notice!

Now the time has come to have the original stock revert to its rightful owner, Christian. Other provisions have been made for you, Samantha, and, needless to say, you are now a very wealthy woman.

Thank you, dear girl, for caring for an old woman. Let your first daughter carry my name.

Remember me,
Gemini

When Samantha looked up through her tears, it was to see the lawyer smiling fondly down at her. "It seems the old matchmaker has had her way."

"Yes, Mr. Carpenter. Gemini Delaney was a wise and wily lady."

"I can see you're not in the mood to have me read the entire addendum to you," he said kindly, offering her a tissue to dry her eyes. "We can go over it at your convenience. By the way, the dividends for the stock that you've already received are yours to keep. I hope you invest them wisely."

"Well, actually, Mr. Carpenter, I didn't cash the check. I gave it to Mr. Delaney in a manila envelope to hold in his office safe. Perhaps you should call him and tell him I'm returning it. I never had any intention of keeping the money. I know Gemini meant well, but I really can't accept it. I tried to explain all of this to your uncle, but he kept getting me confused with a man, and he has a definite hearing problem. I gave up trying to explain, thinking it would all work out. I don't want a cent from the estate. I want you to tell Christian that for me, and I want you to do it today.''

"Are you saying what I think you're saying?'' the young lawyer asked incredulously. "Don't you think you should be the one to tell Mr. Delaney? After all, he is your husband.''

"I want it to come from you, and I want you to explain the mixup.''

"Mrs. Delaney, this is very unorthodox. First, your husband comes in here and tells me he wants things one way, and then you come in and tell me you want it another way. Do you think you could get together and arrive at some sort of mutual agreement so I'm not forced to do double work? We're rather short-staffed here right now.''

"What did Christian tell you to do?'' Sam asked fearfully. Maybe she wasn't going to get the chance to broil that rare steak, after all.

"To make a long story short, he wants you to have half—fifty percent—of the Delaney estate. Half of everything. Now, you tell me you want nothing, not even the dividends."

"That is it, exactly. And I want you to make Mr. Delaney aware of my intentions before he comes home to dinner tonight."

"I'll certainly do my best, Mrs. Delaney, but your husband has a mind of his own, and he was most adamant this morning when he told me his wishes."

"Thank you for your time," Sam said, rising and holding out her hand.

"Goodbye, Mrs. Delaney, and I also want to thank you for braving that white stuff out there. How did you get here?"

"I walked." Sam smiled.

"I'll get on this right away, and perhaps by the time your husband gets home tonight, we'll have it all settled to your satisfaction."

"Is there anything else, Mr. Carpenter?" Sam asked hesitantly.

"David. Call me David. As a matter of fact, there is. I hope you'll include my name on the guest list for the wedding."

"Wedding?" Sam asked, puzzled.

"Yes. Mr. Delaney and I discussed it at great length this morning." The lawyer paused to smile, a hint of a flush reddening his ears. "To quote your husband, Mrs. Delaney, he wants to do everything up right, twice, to make sure you don't get away."

Sam gasped, "Christian said that!" Her heart was beating trip-hammer fast. All the love she had locked away in a tiny part of her breast swelled and grew and burst forth, shining in her eyes.

"I seem to be missing something here," David Carpenter murmured quietly, a frown on his face. "I hope I haven't let any cats out of the bag."

"Cats! Cats!" Sam laughed. "All because of the cats!"

"I beg your pardon, Mrs. Delaney, I'm afraid I don't understand..."

"I'm having trouble with it myself, David," Sam called over her shoulder as she sailed out of the lawyer's office, her feet barely touching the floor.

Her first stop was a supermarket where she picked out the biggest steak she could find. Ingredients for a salad and some baking potatoes. Something for dessert, and an apron. If there was one thing a new bride needed besides perfume, it was an apron, and not necessarily in that order.

It was mid-afternoon before Sam made it back to her apartment, slipping and sliding, carrying two full bags of groceries.

She hung her coat in the tiny closet and immediately set about cleaning the apartment. She cleaned out the grate and added two logs to the fireplace. With machine-gun speed she whipped off the bed sheets and replaced them with fresh ones. A quick once-over in the bathroom and a new bath mat and her house was in order. While the tub filled with luxurious, scented steam, she retreated to the kitchen and began her preparations for dinner. The porterhouse steak was thick and a beautiful beefy-red. Deftly, she added a little tenderizer and sprinkled on a few spices. She set the broiler pan on top of the stove and moved on to the baking potatoes, which were long and perfectly shaped. The vegetables were perfection as she rinsed them under cold water. Her only cop out had been the frozen deep-dish apple pie made by the renowned Mrs. Smith. The pie could bake along with the potatoes, and at the last minute she would slip the steaks under the broiler.

She was married, really married. Her hands trembled as she slid the frozen pie onto a cookie sheet. This would be the first meal she cooked for her husband. "Gemini, you fox, this was what you angled for from the beginning. Wherever you are, I hope you know that your plan worked. And I really wouldn't have given him the cats. I just said that because I was angry. I said I would take care of them, and I will."

Sam fished around in the market bag and withdrew the apron she had purchased in the dime store. At best, it was useless. As big as a handkerchief and sheer as gossamer. A delicate ruffle around the edges led into the tie that was of bonbon proportions. She just knew Christian would love it.

The clock in her sunshine kitchen of yellow and orange read six-forty-five. The table was set to perfection; the candle was waiting to be lighted. At precisely, six-fifty-eight her doorbell chimed. Quickly, she patted at the ridiculous apron—no not ridiculous; sexy—and raced to the door. She flung open the door and fell into Christian's arms. This was where she wanted to be, where she belonged. For now, forever.

"Hey, it's cold out here and it's snowing! Can I come in?" Christian said huskily. Without loosening his hold on her, he managed to slip out of his heavy jacket. "I like your apron." He grinned.

"I knew you would; that's why I bought it!"

"Come here," he said, drawing her closer.

Sam buried her head against his broad chest, burrowing against him. "I have to put the steak under the broiler. Everything else is ready," she sighed.

"Steak?" Christian said in a nonplussed tone.

"David Carpenter said you wanted a steak and that you liked it rare. That's what I'm making for dinner. Did you change your mind? Did David make a mistake?" Sam asked anxiously, not wanting anything to spoil this first dinner for the two of them.

"No! I did say that, but the last thing I want to do right now is eat. Right now, all I want is to make love to you. All through the night until I know every inch of you. And you can start pleasing me by taking off that apron."

Sam giggled. "But what about the steak? I paid seven dollars and forty-three cents for that piece of meat," she whispered against his ear.

"Orion, there are some things more important than eating—and this is one of them." Deftly, he picked her up and headed for the kitchen. Sam wiggled and reached down to turn off the broiler.

"See that pie I baked for you? I was going to lie and say I spent all afternoon slaving over a hot oven. It was one of those frozen creations that are supposed to mesmerize a man."

"What am I going to do with you? Didn't anyone ever tell you that women are supposed to be a mystery to men? You've given away all of your secrets, and this is only the second day we've been together as husband and wife. What am I going to do with you?"

"For starters," Sam said softly, "you can whisper my name the way you did last night, and then we'll think of something after that."

* * * * *

A romantic collection that
will touch your heart....

To Mother with Love '93

Diana Palmer
Debbie Macomber
Judith Duncan

As part of your annual tribute to
motherhood, join three of Silhouette's
best-loved authors as they celebrate the
joy of one of our most precious gifts—
mothers.

Available in May at your favorite retail outlet.

Only from ▼ Silhouette®

—where passion lives.

Silhouette Books
is proud to present
our best authors,
their best books...
and the best in
your reading pleasure!

Throughout 1993, look for exciting books
by these top names in contemporary
romance:

CATHERINE COULTER—
Aftershocks in February

FERN MICHAELS—
Nightstar in March

DIANA PALMER—
Heather's Song in March

ELIZABETH LOWELL
Love Song for a Raven in April

SANDRA BROWN
(previously published under
the pseudonym Erin St. Claire)—
Led Astray in April

LINDA HOWARD—
All That Glitters in May

When it comes to passion,
we wrote the book.

▼ *Silhouette*®

WHERE WERE YOU WHEN THE LIGHTS WENT OUT?